"You must be Sergeant Caruso. Welcome to Black Arrow."

He lifted his shades slowly, his gaze locking onto hers. Silver's heart did a tight little tumble. Fringed by soft, black lashes, his eyes were a warm liquid brown. But the lines that fanned out from them spoke of something she recognized all too well.

This man had been hurt. But he was pretending otherwise.

Strong fingers closed around hers as he clasped her hand firmly. Silver's pulse raced. Sergeant Gabriel Caruso oozed danger—not for Black Arrow, but for her personally. And by the sharp flicker in his eyes, she saw he'd felt something, too.

A Mountie was the last person on this earth she needed to be attracted to. Especially a homicide cop.

Not with her dark secret.

Dear Reader,

The North attracts a free-spirited and disparate sort. It's wild country, a last frontier—a harsh and beautiful place where temperatures can plunge to -58° Fahrenheit, where inhabitants must endure long periods without sunlight, a sense of isolation and a culture foreign to most of us.

Those who weren't born to the North are often lured above the 60th parallel in search of something—gold, silver, meaning. Adventure.

Others go to escape—the law, past relationships, bad mistakes, themselves.

But although the area is vast, it's not an easy place to hide. The inhospitable terrain bonds unlikely allies, and the social circles are in fact small. Mistakes can mean death, and the loneliness forces people to look inward, to dig deep and find their true mettle. The North forms larger-than-life characters, larger-than-life adventure…and to me, it inspires romance.

I hope you enjoy the first book in my WILD COUNTRY series—tales from this vast land, and the characters it shapes.

Loreth Anne White

LORETH ANNE WHITE

Manhunter

Silhouette®
Romantic
SUSPENSE

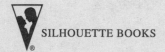 SILHOUETTE BOOKS

ISBN-13: 978-0-373-27607-3
ISBN-10:   0-373-27607-9

MANHUNTER

Copyright © 2008 by Loreth Beswetherick

Visit Silhouette Books at www.eHarlequin.com

Printed in U.S.A.

Books by Loreth Anne White

Silhouette Romantic Suspense

Melting the Ice #1254
Safe Passage #1326
The Sheik Who Loved Me #1368
*The Heart of a Mercenary #1438
*A Sultan's Ransom #1442
Seducing the Mercenary #1490
*The Heart of a Renegade #1505
**Manhunter #1537

*Shadow Soldiers
**Wild Country

LORETH ANNE WHITE

As a child in Africa, when asked what she wanted to be when she grew up, Loreth said a spy...or a psychologist, or maybe marine biologist, archaeologist or lawyer. Instead she fell in love, traveled the world and had a baby. When she looked up again she was back in Africa, writing and editing news and features for a large chain of community newspapers. But those childhood dreams never died. It took another decade, another baby, and a move across continents before the lightbulb finally went on. She didn't *have* to grow up. She could be them all—the spy, the psychologist and all the rest—through characters. She sat down to pen her first novel...and fell in love.

She currently lives with her husband, two daughters and their cats in a ski resort in the rugged Coast Mountains of British Columbia, where there is no shortage of inspiration for larger-than-life characters and adventure.

Prologue

Naked as the day he was born and smeared head to toe with slate-gray river mud, he crawled up the slope, circling above the cabin, careful not to stand in case he was seen from below when lightning flashed.

The night was black and evil, rain slashing horizontally, wind ripping branches and crashing them down to the forest floor, rivers rising and breaking banks.

There would be dogs soon, he knew. And he was leaving a heavy trail of blood.

But tonight the weather was his friend.

He flattened himself into the wet loam, his breathing ragged as he studied the small cabin in the clearing below, the whites of his eyes stark against his mud camouflage.

Lightning cracked open the sky, and for a brief moment the darkness split, revealing a monochromatic snapshot of the churning gray river beyond the cabin, giant logs spinning violently among bobbing flood debris.

Then the image was gone.

He waited for a second for his vision to readjust, then approached the cabin slowly on hands and knees, creeping round to the side with no windows.

Rain leaked into his eyes and blood continued to gush from the ragged bullet trough across his left thigh.

Pain was his friend, he told himself. Adrenaline was his friend.

Twelve months in maximum security might have blunted the brutal edge of his massive physique, but not the steel of his mind. Being a prisoner of war had trained him for this.

U.S. military black ops had trained him for this.

His art was combat. Tracking. Evasion. Infiltration. Torture. He was a killing machine.

A human hunter.

He inched around the cabin, peered up into a window. He needed clothes. Equipment. A needle. Thread. Disinfectant. Then he needed to make it appear as if he'd drowned in that river while he was heading south for the Canadian-U.S. border.

But he was really going north, to the Yukon. To the small town of Black Arrow Falls where they were sending Gabriel Caruso, the cop who had put him behind bars.

He wanted that Mountie.

The game isn't over yet, Caruso, he told himself. It's not over until one of us dies.

He found a rusted piece of crowbar buried in the grass. Ducking round to the front door, he quickly jimmied the bar between the lock and the door. One sharp jerk, and the lock splintered away from wood.

He stilled. Listened. The heavy iron fisted at his side, he entered the dark cabin.

The real hunt had just begun.

Chapter 1

Black Arrow Falls
Northern Yukon
Population 389

Silver Karvonen swung her hunting rifle round to her back and hefted a bag of feed into the bed of her red pickup, three husky-wolf crossbreeds milling around at her feet. The bag landed with a dull thud, releasing a cloud of fine gray glacial dust.

Everything was dry. Hot. The leaves had turned brittle gold and the bush was redolent with the scents of late autumn, the air adrift with the white fluff of fireweed gone to seed, blowing on the hot afternoon breeze like summer snow.

Silver swiped the perspiration from her brow with the back of her wrist as she returned to the shade of the airstrip hangar for another load.

Although the night had brought fresh skiffs of snow to the

high granite peaks, the mid-September afternoon had spiked to sweltering temperatures. Even so, it would be a mere matter of days before snow blew into the dusty streets of Black Arrow Falls itself, blanketing the small northern town for six months of long, dark and isolated winter.

Silver didn't mind. She liked winter best.

That's when her work at the hunting lodge was over. Time was her own, and she could run with her dogs.

But right now she was tired, and in need of a shower. She'd been tracking a large grizzly sow for the better part of the day, arising when the grass was still stiff with night frost and the trail easy to follow.

She'd set off at first light with her three favorite hounds, moving quickly, wanting to sight the grizzly one last time before nightfall.

Silver had encountered her quarry in a wide valley colored rust with fall berry scrub. She'd observed her bear quietly from up high on a ridge, downwind of the animal.

The omnivore was massive—maybe five hundred pounds, close to her peak hibernation weight, sunlight glinting on a majestic golden-brown coat that rippled over powerful haunches as she foraged along the valley bottom.

Within a week the bear would be digging a den oriented leeward of prevailing winter winds. She'd enter it a few days later when she scented the first winter storms in the air. Hopefully her troubles would then be over.

This grizzly had mauled a British hunter last week.

Silver had been contracted by the understaffed conservation office to hunt—and shoot—her.

But after tracking and watching the sow for the last three days, Silver did not think she was a predatory man killer. The British hunting party had alleged one story, but the tracks had told Silver another.

From the evidence around the attack site, Silver deduced that the men had encountered the sow shortly after she'd been injured in a fight with an aggressive and mature male grizz who'd just killed her male cub-of-the-year.

The sow had fought off the much larger male but lost her cub and a claw on her left front paw in the process.

From that point Silver had dubbed her Broken Claw, and as always, she began to emotionally connect with the creature she was tracking.

Injured and severely stressed, Broken Claw had been guarding her cub's dead body when the hunters had startled her along a narrow trail high on the rocky outcrop. She had charged the group in an attempt to warn the hunters back. The men fled, triggering chase.

The grizz swiped at the last hunter who'd been spared death only because the power of her blow had sent him tumbling like a rag doll down the sharp scree of a narrow ravine; he'd later been airlifted out. This much Silver knew from the conservation officer's report. The scuffs and tracks, the remains of the cub, told her the rest.

Retreating quietly from the rock ridge with her dogs, Silver had made up her mind this afternoon to let the bear be.

There was no way she was going to kill that bereaved mother to satisfy a misguided lust for vengeance. Things had played out as nature had intended. Wild justice, she called it.

Silver understood what it meant to lose a child to an aggressive male. She knew just how far a mother would go to eliminate a threat.

It didn't make her a killer.

In a few days the healing snows would come, and Broken Claw would be asleep in her den.

She lifted another sack of horse feed from the airstrip hangar, lugged it to her truck, perspiration dampening her T-shirt as she launched it into the back. One more to go, and then she'd be done with the delivery Air North had flown in for her that morning.

But she stilled at the distant drone of a plane. Silver squinted up into the hazy sky and saw the small twin-engine prop used by the Royal Canadian Mounted Police emerge shimmering between gaps in the massive snow-capped peaks.

The new cop, she thought, shading her eyes, watching as the plane banked around Armchair Glacier, coming in for the steep descent necessitated by the valley formation and prevailing crosswinds.

In a community this small, everyone already knew the new Mountie's name—Sergeant Gabriel Caruso. Big shot detective from British Columbia.

This would be the first time an RCMP officer with the rank of sergeant had been posted to this tiny self-governing First Nations community—one of the only two Yukon communities with absolutely no road access—and already everyone was wondering why the Mounties were sending a veteran homicide cop to Black Arrow Falls where nothing much happened beyond a marauding moose, an overturned snow machine, or a domestic spat spurred by bootleg liquor.

Harry Peters, chief of the tiny Black Arrow Nation for which the town was named, had explained to his people that the RCMP were enlarging what was traditionally a three-man detachment because of the new copper mine opening about 150 miles south of here. The new mine would bring a new road next summer. And more people to town.

More trouble, too, thought Silver.

The wheels of the plane touched dirt with a sharp snick, and the craft bounced along the gravel runway, trailing a cone of silt, coming to a stop across from her as the props slowed.

Silver leaned back against the warm hood of her truck, hooking the ankle of one boot over the other, swatting at a cloud of tiny black insects as she watched the cop alight from the plane. His formidable size and stature struck her instantly, and her pulse quickened.

He hesitated briefly at the top stair, taking in his surroundings, dark hair gleaming in the sun. Then he shouldered his gear, coming quickly down the rest of the steps and striding confidently toward the hangar where she was standing. She noticed that he favored his right leg slightly and was trying to hide that fact.

It spoke of pride, or vanity maybe. Or perhaps an unwillingness to admit weakness or failure.

Newcomers were always a diversion, and Silver studied this one unabashedly, reading his posture just as she read creatures in the wild. And as he neared, she could see right off that there was something different about this *cheechako*.

Something dangerous.

He telegraphed the classic command presence of a cop, walking with a tall, broad-shouldered gait, his spine ramrod straight, jaw held proud. But there was an additional edginess about him that the neat yellow stripes down the sides of his pressed RCMP pants, and the polished gleam of his weapons belt and boots, couldn't quite hide.

Trapped inside that crisp Mountie uniform was a renegade, someone gone a little wild. Someone who might have a problem with authority.

The man was trouble.

If Silver were picking a dog for her team, she'd be leery of one with body language like his. He didn't look like a team player. He looked unpredictable.

His rank and bio suddenly made sense—the RCMP had sent damaged goods. And what better place to dump a problem cop than the backwaters of Black Arrow Falls, just south of the Arctic circle?

A whisper of irritation and wariness laced through her instinctive interest in the man.

Silver had bad experience with the federal force. The Mounties had let her down when she'd needed them most.

And they had the power to put her away.

She turned away from him as he approached, ordering her dogs to sit with a soft whisper as she bent to lift the last feedbag into her truck. Her hounds regarded him warily as he neared.

"Need a hand?" His voice rippled like dark wild honey over her hot skin. Silver froze, startled by the shock waves he'd sent through her system.

Her answer was to tighten her grip on the sack of feed and heft the bag up, dumping it into the truck herself with a heavy thud. She slapped the tailgate closed with a dull clunk before locking it into place, trying to tamp down the energy crackling through her body before facing him again.

She turned, dusting her palms against her jeans and swinging her long, heavy black ponytail back over her shoulder. "Hey," she said, extending her hand, unable to read his eyes behind the mirrored shades. "You must be Sergeant Caruso. Welcome to Black Arrow Falls."

He lifted his shades slowly, his gaze locking onto hers, and Silver's heart did a tight little tumble. She hadn't anticipated eyes like that. They were a warm liquid brown, fringed by soft black lashes, but the lines that fanned out from them—the way they etched into his ruggedly handsome features and olive skin—spoke of something she recognized all too well.

This man had been roughed up, hurt. But he was pretending otherwise.

Strong fingers closed around hers as he clasped her hand firmly, the charge as his skin connected with hers instant. Silver's pulse raced.

Sergeant Gabriel Caruso oozed danger—not for Black Arrow Falls but for her personally.

Silver had not experienced this kind of visceral response to a man since a brutal assault and rape five years ago had emptied her of all feeling. She'd remained hollow since then, beginning to think she was incapable of ever feeling physical lust again. And by the sharp flicker in his eyes, she saw he'd felt something, too.

A quiet fear snaked through her belly.

A Mountie was the last person on this earth she needed to be attracted to. Especially a homicide cop.

Not with her dark secret.

Not with the cold case files buried in the Black Arrow Falls detachment drawers.

She valued freedom too much.

"I'm Silver," she said, words suddenly dry like dust in her mouth, an irrational urge to flee surging through her. But she held her ground, outwardly calm. Flight triggered chase. It showed weakness.

Silver hated appearing weak.

And she wanted to do nothing that would pique the new cop's curiosity, nothing at all that might send him digging back into the old murder files.

His eyes swept over her, taking in her rifle, the brutal hunting knife sheathed at her hips, her dusty scuffed boots, the faded and torn jeans.

He was reading her, thought Silver. Sizing her up just as she had done to him, taking in his new surroundings, yet he gave nothing away in his features. This was a man from whom a person didn't keep secrets. The instinct to pull away intensified as fear rustled deeper into her belly, the raw kind of fear that came from being a so-called criminal faced with the penetrating eyes of law enforcement.

The kind of fear that came with the surprising reawakening of her body.

Gabe felt her hand in his, noting the bracelet of leather knotted with small colorful beads around her slender wrist. She wore no ring.

He was conscious of rings. Engagement rings.

He couldn't help seeking the small circle of promise on other women's fingers. A promise a killer had denied him. His chest tightened as he recalled the reasons that had brought him here.

She answered his handshake with a startlingly firm grip despite her willowy stature. Her palms were rough, not like the hands of any women he knew.

Even Gia's—his hardworking, no-nonsense, cop fiancée's hands—had been softer. Yet there was something alluring—challenging even—in Silver's assertive grip.

She met his gaze just as directly, her indigo eyes showing an unveiled interest that sent a tingle down his spine.

The startling color of her almond-shaped eyes stood out dramatically against skin the color of burnt sienna. Her cheekbones were equally exotic, angled high, and her sleek black hair was harnessed into a waist-length braid that shimmered in the sunlight as she moved, reminding Gabe of the multi-faceted rainbows hidden in a raven's feathers.

Gabe had never seen a woman quite like Silver.

And a woman had never looked at him with quite the same intensity. Her eyes cut into him like blue lasers, as if she could see straight through to his soul. It was as intimate as it was provocative, and he felt his energy instinctively darken and hum.

"He's on his way," she said, sliding her hand free from his grasp, backing away, her voice husky, low. Smooth. The kind of voice that made a guy think about whiskey and sex, things Gabe hadn't thought about in a long time.

"Pardon?" he said, distracted.

Silver swung open the cab door of her truck and whistled for her dogs to jump in the back. "I said your constable is on his way. He'd have waited until he saw your plane come in. No rush up here. There he is now—" She jutted her chin to indicate a column of gray dust churning along the distant dull-green tree line beyond the runway.

Gabe squinted, making out the distinctive white truck with bold RCMP stripes and logo as the police four-by-four neared.

"That would be Donovan." She climbed into her truck as she spoke, folding those impossibly long denim-clad legs under the steering wheel of her cab.

Gabe replaced his shades, uneasy with his own physical reaction to this unusual woman, not wanting her to read it. She seemed to be reading everything.

"Mostly he uses the ATVs." She slammed the door, leaning her elbow out the open window as she started the ignition. "Can't go far with that vehicle in a town with roads that don't lead anywhere." She threw him a final glance, or was it a challenge?

"How long is your posting? Two years?" she asked, a shrewd look in her eyes.

He was glad for his shades. "You've only just welcomed me, and you're ready to see me leave?" She wouldn't be the first to want to see the back of him.

Amusement whispered over her lips. "Everyone goes back to where they came from, Sergeant. Sooner than later. Cops included. Most come north of 60 looking for something, you know? Gold, silver, escape, freedom. Some don't even know what it is they're searching for." She shifted her truck into gear. "Sometimes they find it. Sometimes they don't. But eventually they all do go back."

She smiled, an incredible slash of bright white teeth against her brown skin, a wild glimmer of light in her eyes. "Apart from a few special ones."

Then she hit the gas, leaving him standing in a cloud of silt, her wolf dogs yipping with excitement in the back.

Gabe couldn't help thinking the woman was like this place—strikingly gorgeous and seemingly open, yet hostile to those unequipped to deal with the terrain.

She'd left his blood racing.

And for the first time in what had been a very long year, Gabe thought that maybe he didn't want to die after all.

Chapter 2

Gabe's bitterness resurfaced as soon as the RCMP truck drew to a stop and a young, eager, and smiling Constable Mark Donovan stepped out to greet him.

Gabe reached forward to shake his hand, thinking how much he'd been like Donovan once, filled with idealistic notions of a bright future, of what it meant to be a Mountie, to *maintain le droit* across this vast country in a tradition dating back to the 1800s.

As a young boy growing up in the Italian quarter of Vancouver, Gabe had devoured heroic tales of the Northwest Mounted Police sent to crush the U.S. whiskey peddlers controlling the prairies. After that came the Klondike gold rush with hordes stampeding from Alaska over the Chilkoot Trail, crossing into Canada's harsh, frigid and unforgiving Yukon, with the most famous Mountie of all, Sam Steele—Lion of the Yukon—guarding the pass in his red serge, wide-brimmed Stetson and high browns.

The legends of those Mounties staking claim to the great North, keeping order and saving lives, were the stuff that had fueled young Gabriel Caruso's boyhood dreams and driven him to become a cop.

Ironic, he thought, to be posted to Yukon soil now that he was facing the end of his policing road after 17 years of exemplary service, now that his childhood dream had been darkened by the grit of realism.

Working the major crimes unit in a tough urban centre could do that to you. But it was a more recent incident that had sunk his soul.

On passing his sergeant's exam two years ago, Gabe had accepted a promotion as sergeant of operations at Williams Lake in British Columbia's interior. He'd have preferred to stay in major crimes as a senior investigator, but he'd taken the more administrative job because Gia, the woman he wanted to spend the rest of his life with, had been posted as a new corporal to the Williams Lake detachment.

But a shocking run-in with Kurtz Steiger—a psychopathic serial killer the media had dubbed the Bush Man—had ended Gia's life shortly after they'd gotten engaged.

And life as Gabe knew it was over.

Now, a year later, he was here. Alone. About as far north as you could hang a Mountie out to dry, facing a looming godforsaken winter of 24-hour darkness, endless snow, and a bleak future. Steiger's words slithered back into his brain.

I saw her eyes, Sergeant. I watched her die. I was the last thing she saw, and it was a great pleasure...

Gabe's jaw tightened and his head began to pound.

Shaking Constable Donovan's hand, he tried to remind himself he'd wanted this. He'd asked for this remote post.

He'd needed to get out from under the never-ending media scrutiny, away from Gia's family, his own relatives. Away from his own overwhelming burden of guilt.

He'd been through the critical incident stress debriefings,

through the private specialists, been through the physical therapy, the hearings, the protracted internal investigation, his every action examined and requestioned.

And his force had stood by him. They all said he'd done what any good cop would have done.

Trouble was, Gabe didn't believe it.

He should have guessed when they'd had no response from a member on a supposedly routine call to a disturbance at a Quonset hut on a farm on the outskirts of town that it could be a trap. There had been claims the Bush Man had recently been seen in the wilderness around town, but although the Williams Lake detachment was put on alert, these sorts of sightings were not unusual. The Bush Man had achieved near-mythical status, and civilians had been sighting him in the wilds from Saskatoon to Prince Rupert since his first murder.

Kurtz Steiger, a consummate survivalist and U.S. Special Forces soldier trained in unconventional warfare behind enemy lines, had been defying a federal manhunt in the Canadian wilderness for almost three years following his escape from U.S. court martial for heinous war crimes in the Middle East and Africa.

He'd fled north into the Canadian Rockies where he'd begun killing and torturing again—living for the thrill of the hunt, picking hunters off in the woods, raping and terrorizing campers and hikers, breaking into remote cottages, and living off the land.

The military had been called in, and people in rural towns lived in mounting fear as the notorious killer continued to elude and taunt law enforcement.

But then the Bush Man had simply disappeared, gone quiet after a horrific killing spree near Grande Cache north of Jasper. People speculated that he'd fled over the Rockies, crossing the Cariboo Mountains and then perhaps gone down to Bowron Lake, or Wells Gray Provincial Park. But the terrain was hostile, and talk turned to suggestions he might finally have perished.

Until a hunter had gone missing near Horsefly.

There was no evidence that the hunter had been killed, but the rumors started again. With them came fear. And the expected sightings.

A logger said he thought he may have picked up the Bush Man hitching between Quesnel and Williams Lake. Two German hikers believed they'd glimpsed him north of town. Again, nothing was substantiated, but Mounties in the region were put on alert.

Then came the call to the Quonset hut. Two constables responded, went radio silent.

In the teeth of an unseasonably early snowstorm, darkness falling, the Williams Lake staff sergeant had dispatched every member at his disposal, including Gabe, his operations sergeant, while he'd called in the Emergency Response Team—the Mountie SWAT equivalent—from Prince George. The military was also put on standby.

But the blizzard drove down. The ERT guys were socked in, hours away, choppers grounded. And Gabe, as the senior officer on site, had led his members straight into an ambush in the middle of whiteout.

It had been orchestrated by Kurtz Steiger. He had one officer and one civilian down inside, and one constable hostage.

Gabe was backed into a corner, with no help in sight for hours, perhaps days.

And somehow the bastard knew.

He knew that Gia belonged to him.

He'd been playing them *all,* lurking around town for God knew how long, watching, learning, searching for his next thrill, and the ambush was it.

Gabe should have done anything but send Gia round the back of the Quonset hut with a young constable, where the Bush Man had come barreling out, blazing a pump-action shotgun as the hut had exploded in a ball of fire behind him.

Steiger had felled Gia and Gabe's constable, taking time to

get down and look into Gia's eyes as she died in the snow while the other officers, stunned by the explosion, battled through the blaze to find their fallen comrades and the civilian victim.

Steiger had then fled into the woods on a snowmobile.

Blinded by rage and adrenaline, Gabe had given chase, finally running him down and wounding him. In the bloody battle that had ensued, Steiger had managed to crush Gabe's leg by pinning him between the snowmobile and a tree before Gabe tasered him several times. Steiger, passing in and out of consciousness, had looked directly into Gabe's eyes, and smiled, told him that he'd enjoyed watching Gia die. Gabe had been about to slit the bastard's throat with his own hunting knife just as one of his corporals arrived on scene, saving him from an act that would have cost him his badge had there been a witness. The notorious Bush Man was finally taken into custody.

But the cost was high. And personal.

The RCMP, while a paramilitary organization, was different from the military in one vital sense. Soldiers were trained to take life. But a Mountie lived and breathed to *preserve* life. Lethal force was only used as a last resort, and only to protect life under immediate threat. This was so powerfully ingrained in the Mountie psyche that when things turned violent—when people got killed—it was close to impossible to get over.

Especially when the lives lost were those of fellow members. Especially when that fellow member was your fiancée.

And her death was your fault.

But the internal investigation had cleared Gabe. The metal pin in his leg didn't hurt so badly anymore, and physical therapy had helped him walk again. The funerals in Ottawa were long over, and the shrinks had okayed Gabe for active service.

But they didn't know.

They didn't know how close Gabe had come to killing Steiger even once the bastard had been incapacitated. They didn't know that Gabe didn't trust himself with his own gun anymore.

He'd never told the psychologists how quickly his rage flared now. How he had to bite down to stop clearing leather with his 9 mm. That he'd become his own worst enemy.

Perhaps he should have told them, but they would have sidelined him. And he'd needed to work to stay half-sane.

But until he figured some things out, Gabe thought it best to go work someplace where he could lie low, where the crime rate was virtually zero.

Where he couldn't goddamn hurt anyone else.

Like Black Arrow Falls.

A deeply buried part of Gabe figured he might just disappear up here. Walk into the wilderness with a fishing rod, maybe dissolve into the fabric of the mountains. Never come back. Forcing himself to embrace living was going to be his ultimate test.

"So this is the Black Arrow Falls detachment," Donovan was saying as he wheeled the RCMP vehicle into a gravel parking lot behind a rustic log building atop which a red-and-white Canadian flag flapped in the warm wind.

Gabe struggled to focus as he followed Donovan into the building.

His sole absolution was that he'd put Steiger behind bars.

It was the only way he could justify his sacrifices. The only way he could accept the loss of Gia's life, the other officers' lives.

Steiger would not kill again.

"And this is Rosie Netro's desk," said Donovan, showing Gabe into the reception area of the tiny RCMP detachment. It was a far cry from where he'd worked in the city. Even Williams Lake was sophisticated compared to this.

"Rosie's one of our two civilian clerks who handle dispatch and admin. She's off-duty now, usually works nine to five weekdays. Tabitha Charlie is our weekend dispatcher, a fairly recent addition, but she's off on maternity leave."

Donovan smiled his clean, earnest smile in his square jaw. "Baby should be along any day now."

Donovan waited for a reaction from Gabe, some platitude. A smile, a nod, perhaps.

Gabe registered it was a great thing, a birth. But he couldn't seem to make himself respond.

His reaction was buried down somewhere in his repertoire of expected and acceptable social behaviors, but he didn't have the inclination to set it free. *Emotional dissonance,* the shrinks had called it.

It had grown out of his habit of compartmentalizing things as a homicide cop, and now he seemed to have locked himself down permanently somewhere inside. It was the only way he'd gotten through this past year. It had kept him alive. But it sure as hell wasn't living.

Donovan turned his eyes away, a subtle but visible shift in his demeanor. "And this is where we all sit. Constable Annie Lavalle at that desk over there. That's my station," he pointed. "And that's Constable Stan Huong's desk, and that station by the window will be for the new member, Cade McKenzie. His transfer comes through in a couple of months."

"Where are Lavalle and Huong now?" Gabe asked, surveying the mini-bullpen.

"Huong's on compassionate leave. His mother passed away. We expect him back in two weeks. Lavalle is attending a court case in Whitehorse—hunting violation. She was called to testify. It's her first case. She's fresh out of Depot Division."

A new recruit straight out of the academy. Gabe didn't like the sense of responsibility that gave him. Call him chauvinist, but he didn't want to put another woman in jeopardy. Ever. It went against his grain as much as it was drummed home to him that they were all equal in the force. He was a born protector. That's what had given him the black eyes and broken arm at school when he'd stood up in defense of his kid sister and her friends.

It's what had made him a good cop.

"Name like Lavalle—she Québécoise?" he asked.

"Yeah," said Donovan. "Accent and feisty temper to match."

Gabe grunted. At least there was little to threaten young Constable Annie Lavalle up here in Black Arrow Falls. Apart from wild animals and his own morbidity. He'd have to be careful not to spread the poison—it wasn't fair to these young officers.

"Lockup's down this way." Donovan led Gabe down a hallway. "Interview room is in there, evidence and equipment room over here on the right." He unlocked and swung open a door, revealing shelves with snowmobile helmets, two satellite phones, and other equipment on the left, racks for rifles and shotguns down the centre, and shelves with evidence bags near the back.

"And this is the gym." Donovan squared his shoulders as he opened another door into a small square room furnished with rudimentary weights, a treadmill, and a bike.

It was painted stark white, with a small window. Like a cell. Gabe could imagine snowdrifts piled so high they covered that tiny window. A small fist of tension curled in his stomach. Along with it came a tingle of claustrophobia.

This was going to be tougher than he thought.

This was going to be his prison, his self-inflicted punishment for what went wrong that day.

He wondered now, as he stared at the small room, if he'd ever find his way back, or if Black Arrow Falls really was the end of his road, his permanent rock bottom.

"And this here is your office," Donovan said, moving back into the main room and opening a door into a partitioned-off area. The fist in Gabe's gut curled tighter.

A large window looked out over the desks in the mini-bullpen, while another offered a view out the back of the building over a few tired clapboard houses, leafless scrub, and mountainous wilderness beyond.

He stared silently at the cramped alcove with its ancient computer and regulation desk, his blood beginning to thump steadily in his veins.

"Look," said Donovan suddenly, his cheeks reddening slightly as he spoke. "For the record, I think you made the right decision that day. You got the Bush Man."

"I lost four members and a civilian."

Donovan's cheeks burned redder. Gabe wasn't making it easier for the guy, but his will to ease things for his young constable was buried somewhere inside him, too.

Donovan cleared his throat, his eyes flicking away. "I…should finish showing you around."

"Right."

He cleared his throat nervously again. "As you know, there are no telephone landlines into Black Arrow Falls," he said.

Gabe didn't know. Didn't really care, either. He hadn't bothered to read up on his new detachment beyond the mere basics. The posting had come fast once he'd put in the request. He'd taken it just as fast.

"Phone service and high-speed Internet are provided to the town via satellite dish," Donovan was saying. "The dish picks up the signal, feeds it to individual homes and businesses via local landline. We have our own sat dish and radio antennae mounted on the detachment building. There's a repeater on a hill some miles out, so radio range is fair, but we take a sat phone to communicate with dispatch when we need to head into the bush for any distance."

"Power?"

"Supplied by Yukon Electrical via a diesel-generating plant. Diesel is flown in. Same with regular gas. The Black Arrow Nation runs the gasoline outlet. The Northern Store across the street sells groceries, some dry goods, and provides mail pickup. Mail plane flies in once a week, so does passenger and delivery service with Air North. We have a resident doctor now and two nurses at the community health clinic. The clinic has videoconferencing facilities. Dentist flies in once a month." He snorted. "Most months."

"How long you been here, Constable?" Gabe asked suddenly.

"Five months, sir."

"Your first posting?"

"Second. I was in Faro for two years. I like the north, Sergeant."

Gabe inhaled deeply, reaching for patience. "So it's just you and me for now, then, Constable?"

"And Rosie."

"Yeah." And Rosie. Gabe walked over to the wide window cut into rough-hewn log walls. It looked out over the dusty main street.

"It's not like much happens up here from fall into winter," Donovan offered. "Apart from the odd domestic or drunk disturbance."

That's what ate at Gabe.

Seventeen years had come to this?

"And there was the grizzly attack last week," he said. "That caused a bit of a stir. The file is on your desk."

Gabe wasn't listening, his attention suddenly snared by the woman striding down the road with the hunting rifle slung across her back and a troop of wolf dogs following in her wake.

Silver.

She'd cleaned up, and be damned if she didn't look even more alluring.

Wearing a denim jacket over a white cotton dress that skimmed her tall moccasin-style boots, her long black hair had been released from its braid and swung loose across her back, reaching almost to her butt.

Donovan came to his side. "That's Silver Karvonen. She's the tracker the conservation office contracted to hunt the man killer. Like I said, file is on your desk."

Gabe's eyes shot to Donovan. "Man killer?"

"Well." The constable cleared his throat again, "The grizz didn't actually kill the guy, but the CO said he would have if the hunter hadn't rolled down into the ravine. Bear probably has a taste for human blood now."

Gabe's pulse accelerated slightly. "That your opinion or the CO's?"

He flushed again. "Well, mine, actually, Sergeant."

Gabe glanced back at Silver making her way toward the general store. He hadn't been this interested in *anything* for a long, long time. "You say she's a tracker?"

"One of the best north of 60. Does man tracking, too. They fly her out for some of the real tough search-and-rescue missions, mostly across the North, and especially if there are kids involved. She has a real thing for the lost children. She just won't give up if there's a minor missing."

Intrigue stirred something to life inside him.

"Otherwise she manages the Old Moose Lodge during the summer months for an outfitter based out of Whitehorse. The Old Moose property lies just beyond the town boundaries on the shores of Natchako Lake, where she has a cabin. The outfitters own the hunting concession up here," he said. "And Silver occasionally guides parties who fly in and pay megabucks for the big game."

Gabe watched Silver order her wolf pack to sit before climbing the old wooden stairs of the Northern Store across the street. Gabe knew the population of Black Arrow Falls was 90 percent Black Arrow Gwitchin, a very small subgroup of the Gwitchin Nation that stretched across the Canadian North and into Alaska, but Silver had gotten those laser-blue eyes from somewhere else.

"Karvonen," he said quietly, contemplating the woman vanishing through the store door. "That's not a local name."

"Finnish. Her mother was Black Arrow Gwitchin, but her father was apparently some crazy maverick prospector from

Finland. Most of the prospectors who came up this way were looking for Yukon gold. They called him The Finn, tell me he came looking for silver."

"He ever make a strike?"

"No, but he found a wife and had a kid. That's where she got her name, Silver."

They all come looking for something. Sometimes they don't know what it is.

Gabe almost smiled. So, the prospector got what he came for. He just didn't know it was a family he'd been seeking.

"You up on the local gossip, eh, Constable?"

Donovan shrugged, a grin sneaking across his face, and Gabe felt himself warming to the guy in spite of himself.

But before Donovan could say anything more, the phone on the desk in Gabe's tiny office rang, startling him back to his present predicament.

Donovan jerked his head toward it. "Your direct line, Sergeant. Goes straight through and into voice mail if Rosie's not on duty."

Gabe strode into his new cell, snatched the receiver up to his ear. "Caruso," he barked.

"Gabe, it's Tom."

His RCMP pal from Surrey homicide.

"Tom? How—"

"Where in hell have you been? I've been trying to reach you all day."

"Cell reception out here is a nonexistent luxury."

"You see the news?"

Something inside Gabe quieted at the tone in Tom's voice. "What news?" he said softly.

"The Bush Man—he's on the loose. Kurtz bloody Steiger busted out of max security during the storm last night."

Chapter 3

Gabe's head began to buzz. His fist tightened around the handset.

"How?" he said, barely audibly. "How in hell did he get out?"

"Floodwater was seeping into the underground electrical systems at Kent Institution with this deluge we've been having," said Tom. "Correctional services was sandbagging like crazy while putting together contingency plans to transfer inmates to the Mountain Institution if things got worse."

Gabe could picture it. Kent was in the low-lying area of the Agassiz delta. The neighboring Mountain Institution was on slightly higher ground.

"The water levels rose too fast. Power shorted, backup generator blew as they were trying to switch over. Wardens had to hustle inmates out in the dark."

Gabe's knuckles turned bone-white as he struggled to grasp what he was hearing. Steiger was being held in that institution while lawyers wrangled over his extradition and jurisdictional issues. He vaguely noted Donovan staring at him through the glass. "Go on," Gabe said, words like gravel in his throat.

"Steiger took advantage of the outage, stabbed an inmate with a spoon, it looks like. Sparked a riot in pitch blackness. Two wardens are dead, several others in critical condition. The bastard actually stripped one, put on his uniform, and drove the prison van right out of the main gates of the pen. No one saw it coming—they thought he was one of their own. Steiger dumped the van off the highway near Manning Park. Looks like he ducked into wilderness there, heading south for the U.S. border."

"With a U.S. court martial hanging over his head?"

"Borders don't matter to that guy."

No. *Everything* mattered to Kurtz Steiger. Gabe knew him too well now. He'd studied—memorized—everything the RCMP criminal investigative analysts had come up with. He'd looked right into the monster's eyes himself that snowy night in the woods. He'd almost taken his life. Gabe pinched the bridge of his nose.

"It's all over the news," said Tom. "I...thought you might have heard."

"I'm in the bush, Thomas. North of bloody nowhere."

"The CBC is working up a feature that will air during their regular news slot tonight. I...I wanted to be sure you knew. They'll probably bring up...Gia, and all that."

An inexplicable emotion welled up through Gabe's chest and burned into his eyes. He felt so damn defeated.

Having Steiger behind bars was his way of rationalizing Gia's murder. And the loss of those officers' lives. It was his sole foundation for going forward.

Now it was gone.

He sank down, leaning against his tiny new desk. "Where are they looking for him?" he asked quietly.

"They've got a major manhunt going down in Manning

Park along the U.S. border. Dogs, choppers, military, the works. They're expanding the search over the border into Washington state with the cooperation of U.S. authorities."

"Why?"

A puzzled silence hung for a moment. "That's where his trail leads."

"Steiger doesn't leave a trail," Gabe said even more quietly. "Not unless he wants you to find it."

Tom paused. "They've got him this time, Caruso. He was shot in the prison riot. He left a ton of blood in that van. He's injured and on the run. The dogs are on him."

"Right," said Gabe. Kurtz Steiger could survive anything. It's what he did. Survive. And kill.

"The guy is not superhuman, Gabe. They figure they'll have him in a matter of hours."

"Right," he said again.

Silence hung for several beats. "Is everything okay up there?"

Up there.

It sounded like something Gabe's Roman Catholic mother would say in reference to limbo—that peculiar place where doomed souls were destined to hang between hell and heaven for eternity.

"I'm fine," Gabe lied. "You'll keep me updated, Tom? I…I'm kind of out of the loop right now, and…I'd like to know."

"Hey, it's why I called, buddy."

Gabe hung up, his knuckles bloodless. He flexed his fingers, stared at his hands, then looked up at Donovan who'd moved into the doorway.

"He got out," said Gabe. "The Bush Man."

Donovan's features were grave. "I gathered."

Gabe launched to his feet suddenly, pushing off his desk. "Is there a television set anywhere in this town?"

Donovan eyed him steadily. "We have Internet. You can get the news on—"

"I want a television. I want to see the CBC feature airing on Steiger tonight."

And he wanted a beer. No, a couple of beers. He wanted to drown himself in whiskey—and this was a dry town.

"Mae Anne's diner has TV. She gets the two Yukon channels. There are satellite systems in private homes and one at the Old Moose Hunting Lodge, which is outside the town boundary. They serve a pretty decent meal there, too."

Gabe checked his watch as he stalked through the reception area. Shoving the door open, he stepped out onto the small log porch that fronted the detachment building. He needed air. What he got was a surprise.

The sinking sun had brushed the rugged, snow-capped massifs with a soft peach alpenglow, and the air had turned heavy and cool. Gabe drank it down hungrily as he braced his hands on the wood balcony, heart thudding in his chest. It was so beautiful it had shocked his mind clean for a moment.

"Sergeant?" Donovan said from just inside the door.

Gabe tightened his hands on the balustrade. "What is it, Donovan?" he said quietly, without looking at the man.

"I know you're technically not on duty until tomorrow, but Chief Peters at the band office is expecting you, and I…uh…mentioned you might come around and meet with him this evening."

Black Arrow Nation Chief Harry Peters functioned as a small-town mayor would. His band had contracted the RCMP to police their community, and, as the new sergeant in town, Gabe would need to liaise with Peters in the same way a top cop would work with any local mayor and council.

"Not right now," said Gabe, trying to control the rage mushrooming steadily through him. His short fuse, the murderous impulse that could fill him instantaneously, had become his weakness, a black cancer he couldn't cut out. And he felt it now.

Taking life went against everything that had defined Gabe as an officer of the Royal Canadian Mounted Police force. But if his corporal hadn't arrived when he had the night Gabe had chased Steiger, Gabe knew he would have killed Steiger.

He'd have ripped out the bastard's sick throat with his bare, bloodied hands.

And now he wished he had.

The violent strength that had coursed through Gabe's veins that night had startled him. The sheer power was almost intoxicating.

Locking eyes with Steiger in the woods on that snowy night in Williams Lake just over a year ago had unearthed something dark and atavistic in Gabe.

Because he *still* wanted to kill him.

It was this that made him question whether he really was still fit to wear his red serge and carry a gun.

"I'll see him tomorrow," he said coolly without looking at Donovan. He didn't want to talk to anybody right now. What he needed right now was to find his cabin, get out of his uniform, and find a television and a beer.

He cursed to himself.

They'd locked Steiger in prison, but Steiger had locked him in one, too. Now the bastard was free.

But Gabe was still trapped behind his own damn bars.

In the general store Silver bought rounds for her rifles, a new skinning knife, and she picked up the mail Edith Josie, the owner, was holding for Old Crow. She'd take it out to his camp in a day or so.

Old Crow was a Black Arrow elder and Silver's tracking mentor. She had no idea how old he was—older than time, older than the river, Edith had told her. And Edith was no spring chicken herself.

Whatever his age, to Silver, Old Crow was eternal. A part of her felt he'd always be there for her and that she'd never stop learning from him. It was an education that had begun after her mother had died when Silver was nine. She stopped going to the small Black Arrow school, and her father had been too grief-stricken to make her do otherwise.

Her dad had eventually gotten done with mourning and shacked up with a *cheechako* nurse who took it upon herself to try and homeschool Silver. But during the summers of endless sun Silver would go prospecting in the wilds with her father.

And from time to time she and Finn, as everyone called her father, would run into Old Crow working his traplines, and they'd spend the night in his camp listening to his stories, their campfire shooting orange sparks into the pale sky.

Old Crow could paint pictures in the air with his gnarled brown hands. With a deft sweep of his arm he could show weather patterns, or the animation of a small forest animal. He could tell chapters of a lynx's life from a single footprint in mud, even tell you how to find that lynx—just from the clues in that one track. To a young Silver he was fascinating, a wilderness detective, and she'd started following him around like a lost little bear cub soaking up any stray bit of information she could.

Old Crow had finally, officially, taken Silver under his wing, teaching her how to read the wilderness like an ordinary child might learn to read a book, but he never gave her the information straight. He'd point the way with a riddle, conning her into using her innate curiosity to unravel mysteries with her own effort and skill.

Her own discoveries had thrilled her, and in this way Silver had learned to speak another language, one written right into the fabric of nature. Over time she'd become one of the best trackers in the country, all because of Old Crow. And she'd learned everything else she'd needed to know about life from nature's classroom.

But a good tracker never stops learning, and Silver still thoroughly enjoyed her visits to Old Crow's camp where he lived up on a remote plateau in his teepee, in the old way.

She smiled inwardly as she thanked Edith, tucking his wad of mail into the leather pouch hanging from her shoulder.

Old Crow might prefer living in the traditional way, but he still liked to get his mail from Whitehorse, via plane.

"*Massi Cho,*" she said in the Gwitchin language of the Black Arrow Nation. "*Gwiinzii Edik'anaantii.* Take good care of yourself, Edith."

Edith smiled, her eyes disappearing into brown folds of skin behind her thick glasses as she waved Silver on.

Descending the stairs of the Northern Store, Silver whistled for her dogs as she swung her rifle to a more comfortable position at the centre of her back. But just as she was about to stride up Black Arrow Falls' main road, she caught sight of the new cop standing on the detachment porch, the Canadian flag with its symbolic red maple leaf snapping up over his head against a clear violet sky.

Her heart fluttered awkwardly—and annoyingly—in her chest.

She should have kept right on walking, and she'd have been okay. But she felt him watching, and she made the mistake of looking up at him. Instantly she was snared by the intensity of his gaze.

Silver suddenly forgot how to breathe, a tumult growing inside her coupled with an overwhelming urge to flee. "Hey," she said, stopping instead.

"Any word on that grizz?" His muscled arms braced wide and solid on his detachment banister as his eyes bored down into hers. The posture was proprietary, almost aggressive. Something seemed to have changed in him since she'd met him at the airstrip.

She squinted up at him, disadvantaged by the backlight of the evening sky.

"What about the grizz?" she asked.

"I hear he got a taste of human blood. Donovan tells me you're hunting him."

"The bear's a she, not a he," she said, her voice husky to her own ears. Damn, how could one man have an effect like this on her body, and so quickly? It was beyond her control. And Silver liked—*needed*—to be in control. "Besides, it's not police business."

"Sure it is."

She bristled. "The other officers were content to let the conservation office handle this. And the CO contracted me to take care if it. So it's *my* business."

"I'm not the other cops, Silver."

"Sergeant—" she stepped closer, which further disadvantaged her because now she had to angle her head to look up at him. "The sow was defending her dead cub's body. She was stressed and threatened. Her attack was not predatory. It was in self-defense, so I let her be." Even though she spoke softly, she made sure her words were delivered with authority. Whoever this Caruso was, she was not going to let him go after her bear. That really was her territory, and she couldn't back down.

"She won't become a problem?"

Me or the bear?

The way he said it, the way he was looking at her, she couldn't be sure.

Silver repositioned her rifle and squared her shoulders. "The attack could affect her interaction with humans down the road, so, yes, she could become a problem, but we should give her the winter. Time has a strange way of healing things out here, Sergeant."

His arms tensed, eyes narrowing sharply onto her.

She turned to go, finding her legs like water as she tried to walk up the road, feeling his eyes burning hot into her back.

"Any place a man can get beer round here?" he called out after her.

Silver stilled.

She turned slowly to face him, irony tempting the corners of her mouth into a wry smile. "This is a dry town, officer. I believe it's your job to make sure it stays that way."

"I hear the Old Moose Lodge is out of town limits, and it has a television. I need to watch the news tonight."

She studied him, trying to weigh the paradox that was this man. "It's a public place, Sergeant." She hesitated. "But I'd leave that uniform at home if you plan on drinking in my bar. Wouldn't want Chief Peters and the band council thinking you were officially trying to undermine his efforts to keep our people dry."

Sergeant Gabe Caruso stared at her with a directness that sent another hot tingle into her belly. She turned quickly, calling her dogs to heel.

She concentrated on walking smoothly and calmly down the street. She felt anything but.

The cop was coming to her lodge. Tonight.

He was making her feel things she didn't know she was capable of feeling anymore. That scared her. Because like Broken Claw, Silver was a bereft and wounded mother.

But unlike the grizzly, Silver had actually killed a man.

And if the cop found out, he had the power to put her away for it. For good.

Chapter 4

Gabe tucked his 9 mm into the back of his jeans under his leather bomber jacket and snagged his radio and flashlight off the table. Donovan was on call tonight, and Gabe hadn't yet officially reported for duty, but he took the gear anyway.

He surveyed his tiny cabin for a moment before leaving—his new home for the next two years. It was small, built from thick-hewn logs, the decor utilitarian. A rough table and bench divided the living room from the tiny kitchen area where a woven rag mat rested in front of an old blackened Aga stove. His kitchen window afforded a view of Deer Lake, which was still as glass this evening, reflecting strands of violently pink cirrus in an otherwise pale Nordic sky.

In the living room a small couch faced a stone fireplace, and to its side hunkered one other chair, a great big wingback with stuffing straining to pop out the back. A small bedroom and bathroom led off the main area. His pine bed was covered with a patchwork quilt made by the wife of the corporal who'd been transferred south, a homey touch that seemed to underscore his loneliness.

He couldn't expect more. He'd sold every last thing he and Gia had owned together. The memories stirred by their shared possessions had become unbearable.

He hadn't accumulated anything new, either.

Gabe stepped out onto the porch, locked the door to his tiny log cabin, and stood for a moment, trying to ground himself, his breath misting in the rapidly cooling air.

The earth in front of his humble abode had been freshly tilled, a vegetable garden put to bed for the winter. Gabe could imagine the previous RCMP officer's wife planting food for their table. He could picture the couple using the red canoe that had been pulled up onto the bank and tied under a trembling aspen down near the water. Crisp gold leaves covered the canoe now, a few left clinging at the topmost branches of the tree. One lost its grip and rustled softly to the ground as Gabe watched.

He jacked his shearling collar up around his neck, shoved his hands deep into his pockets, and began the trudge to Old Moose Lodge, wondering how in hell he was actually going to survive six long snowbound months in that little wooden box on the lake, buried under drifts.

Who would care if he didn't?

And he'd still have another winter to endure after this one coming. Where would they send him then?

There wasn't even anywhere else he wanted to go.

Time stretched interminably before him as he crunched along the narrow rutted path, dense spruce and berry scrub closing in on either side, shadows dark in the undergrowth.

He could have taken the ATV, but the lodge was only about six miles from his new home, and he needed to do something physical, or he was going to go insane. But as he walked, a very real sense of being watched crept stealthily over his skin.

He stopped, listened. He couldn't pinpoint why, but something didn't feel right. A slight crunch in the woods sounded suddenly to his right.

He spun, pulse quickening.

Gabe concentrated on the ambient noise of the bush, trying to identify anomalies of sound. Then he heard it again—a crack. Sweat prickled across his brow.

Slowly drawing his weapon, he peered into the arachnid-like shadows of dry willow scrub, twilight toying with definition between shadow and form.

Something rustled sharply again in the dry leaves, and twigs crunched. His pulse kicked up, and his throat turned dry. He removed his flashlight with his free hand, directing the beam into the dense willows, the barrel of his weapon following.

His flashlight caught the quick glint of eyes, then the shape of a large animal seemed to quietly separate itself out from the background, and he found himself gazing into the liquid eyes of a doe, standing still as stone in the shadows.

Gabe's breath whooshed out of him.

Laughing lightly, he reholstered his weapon. The deer skittered back into cover, white tail bobbing, and Gabe laughed again, running both hands over his hair, trembling slightly. He continued along the grassy track, a sudden lightness in his chest.

Yeah, he was still jumpy. But he hadn't shot the damn deer. He still had the jockey of logic to control his quick impulse to shoot.

Looking into the big innocent brown eyes of that doe, feeling a rush of adrenaline in his body that wasn't spawned by malicious human intent, had shifted something fundamental inside Gabe.

Maybe there was hope for him after all.

A split cedar fence lined the approach to the Old Moose Hunting Lodge, a large log structure that hunkered on the shores of the clearest aquamarine lake Gabe had ever seen, a few outbuildings standing off to the side.

A fish eagle circled up high, feathers ruffling on air currents as it craned its neck for prey. Small bats were beginning to flit after mosquitoes just above the water, competing with fish that sent concentric circles rippling through mercurial reflections as they broke the lake surface. The air was heavy and cool, redolent with the scent of pine and the spice of juniper.

Gabe stopped a moment to drink it all in.

Then he saw Silver, leading three horses to a paddock near the shore. There was a wild abandon in her stride, her heavy hair swaying across her back, and she was laughing as her dogs cavorted with a puppy at her side.

Everything inside Gabe quieted.

She looked so free.

It was clear she hadn't realized he was there and that she was being watched. And with mild shock, Gabe realized he *wanted* to watch, quietly, without announcing his presence. There was something about the way she moved that grabbed him by the throat. He was jealous of her freedom, her spirit. It made him feel furtive. Hungry.

But she saw him, and stiffened instantly. He raised his hand to greet her, but she simply pointed toward the main building before continuing down to the paddock with her horses.

Gabe climbed the big log stairs onto a veranda that ran the length of the lodge. Massive bleached moose antlers hung over a heavy double door. He scuffed his boots on the mat and entered the lodge.

A fire crackled in the stone hearth, and two men and a woman chatted at the bar as an Indian barman with a sleek black ponytail down the centre of his back filled a bowl with peanuts. The television set was mounted behind him, a hockey game playing.

Gabe grabbed a stool and bellied up to the bar. He asked for a Molson, and if he could switch to the CBC news channel.

"You the new cop?" asked the barkeep as he slid a cold beer along the counter to Gabe. He was a young and strong man with copper skin and a small silver earring in his left ear.

"Sergeant Gabriel Caruso," Gabe said, holding out his hand.

The trio at the other end of the bar glanced up. Gabe nodded at them, and they tipped their glasses slightly. Not exactly smiles of welcome, thought Gabe. It was the same with Silver. Beneath surface civility he could detect simmering hostility.

"Jake Onefeather," said the barkeep as he flipped to the news channel and handed Gabe the remote.

There was a commercial on. Gabe checked his watch, and tensed. He'd made it just in time. The CBC news logo flashed across the screen, and he bumped up the volume, his mouth already dry, his pulse accelerating. He knew he'd see Steiger's photo. And most likely his own.

And Gia's.

If Tom was correct—that CBC had prepared a news feature—Gabe would likely see file footage from the RCMP funeral where thousands of mourners had come to pay their respects to his colleagues gunned down in the line of duty. Mounties from across the country had stood shoulder to shoulder in a sea of red serge far exceeding the capacity of the Notre Dame Basilica cathedral in Ottawa as the coffins were carried in—one of them holding the body of the woman he'd planned to marry.

The anchor began to speak. But before Gabe could catch a word, a soft and husky female voice brushed like velvet over his skin.

"You'd make a better impression visiting the chief and council than sitting here drinking beer on your first night, you know?" Silver said quietly as she came up behind him.

Abruptly, the competition for Gabe's attention was cleft in

two—the sensually beautiful tracker at his side and the image of Steiger's rugged face filling the screen, pale ice-blue eyes staring coldly at the camera. Steiger's hair was pale, too. Ash blond, shaved short and spiky. By contrast, his skin was olive-toned, his features angular, strong. Handsome, even. Almost mesmerizingly so. And the psychopath knew it.

Gabe's heart began to thud. He felt dizzy. He held up his hand, quieting her, and he made the sound louder. Everyone in the bar looked up in surprise, then fell dead silent as they watched.

Silver stared at the screen in shock as the anchor announced the escape of the Bush Man, and then footage segued to file images of the dead Mounties, and Gabe—the cop who had led the Williams Lake takedown. The cop who had lost his fiancée to a monster.

As a tracker, Silver had been interested in Steiger's story, in how the killer had managed to evade law enforcement for almost three years, but she hadn't put two and two together with the new cop.

Her eyes shot to Gabe.

Suddenly he made sense. She now understood what she'd glimpsed in his eyes.

She'd been right. He *was* damaged goods. Badly damaged.

Silver listened to the news, but she watched him. She was a veteran observer of creatures, human and otherwise. She instinctively noted the way they moved, talked, how their emotions translated into body position, how it made them plant their feet, leave trace. It was in this way that she could often tell the prints of one villager from another without even analyzing why. And more often than not she could tell what they'd been doing, even thinking, at the time they'd left prints.

Right now, in his leather bomber jacket and faded jeans, Gabe Caruso didn't look like a cop. His hair was roughed up, a five o'clock shadow darkened his angled jaw, and his neck muscles corded with aggression. Strong neck. Strong man. She liked what she saw—too much. And again she felt the disturbing warmth spread through her stomach. She didn't feel safe around this man—not at all.

She swallowed the shimmer of anxiety in her chest and pulled up a stool beside him. Closer than was necessary, close enough to feel the tension radiating from him like heat from a desert tarmac. She noted the way he fisted the TV remote in one hand, knuckles white, his beer glass in the other. She thought he might just crush it and wondered if she should remove it or remind him that he was holding glass in his fist.

She slanted her eyes up to the television as another image of Gabe filled the screen. It was a shot taken a year ago of him standing alongside one of the coffins. Propped up by crutches he was dressed in formal RCMP red serge, Stetson at a slight angle atop short-shaved hair, no expression on his face. Just hollow, dark eyes.

The anchor reminded viewers of how the sergeant had pursued Steiger on a snowmobile, racing after him into the teeth of a blizzard on that fateful night. A gunfight and hand-to-hand combat had ensued, seriously injuring Gabe before he'd managed to subdue Steiger using a taser.

And given what they were saying on the news about Gabe having been a fast-climbing career cop who'd taken the sergeant's job in Williams Lake to be with his now-deceased fiancée, Gabe must be seething about this Black Arrow Falls posting. It was a dead end for him.

Silver guessed everything that meant anything to Gabe lay in that coffin in that image. The news feature cut back to the presenter, and Silver felt anger burn through her veins. She knew what that kind of emptiness felt like.

Everything that had meant anything to her was buried under a small cairn of river rocks northwest of town, at Wolverine Gorge. Rocks she'd stacked with her own bloodied hands.

Silver was torn between resentment that the RCMP had sent them someone who didn't want to be here and compassion for a man tormented over the loss of his fiancée and his career. His life. Black Arrow Falls deserved better treatment.

But so did Sergeant Gabriel Caruso.

The RCMP had clearly washed their hands of a dedicated cop, given the résumé they'd just flashed on screen. It sure didn't endear the federal force further to Silver, but suddenly this man wasn't overtly her enemy.

Or was he?

She slanted her eyes back to study his jagged profile. A man like him would now have something to prove. And if the big city homicide detective had nothing better to do in Black Arrow Falls, he just might go sifting through the cold case files.

He might come after *her*.

The news feature was over, but he sat staring blankly at the television screen. Silver didn't know why she did it, but she reached over and quietly pried the remote from his clenched hand.

"They're tracking him wrong," she said as she bumped down the sound, and set the remote on the bar counter.

Gabe's eyes whipped to hers. "What?"

"The Bush Man. They won't get him like that."

He leaned forward suddenly, intense interest narrowing his eyes, energy crackling around him. "Why do you say that?"

"They're combat tracking. It's how you chase down a fugitive on the run."

"That's what he is."

"No," she said softly. "That man is not a fugitive. He's not running. He's a predator. He's hunting again."

"How do you know that?"

"It's what natural-born predators do. They hunt. And when they're injured and backed into a corner, they don't flee. They just become more dangerous. They come at you—attack."

A muscle began to pulse at his jaw. "And how would *you* track him?"

"The same way I track any animal predator."

Gabe shook his head. "No. No way. Steiger is a borderline genius, a strategic combatant. This guy is not an animal. He's a psychopath."

"Which is exactly what makes him like an animal. A very smart and very dangerous one."

Gabe swigged back the rest of his beer, plunked the glass down hard onto the counter, and surged to his feet. "Don't kid yourself, Silver." He pointed to the TV screen. "You could never track that man. Our force hunted him for months. I saw the profilers' reports. I studied every goddamn word. I got inside his sick head." His eyes bored down into hers, giving Silver that strange zing in the base of her spine again. "You'd be dead before you knew it. You may be a good tracker, Silver, but you're no match for Kurtz Steiger. You're not a man hunter."

Her mouth flattened, and her eyes narrowed. "Don't presume to know *anything* about me, Sergeant," she said very quietly as she got to her own feet, meeting his aggressive posture toe to toe, her pulse accelerating. "Do you even know where the word 'game' comes from?"

Uncertainty flickered briefly in his eyes. She held his gaze, well aware of what her blue-eyed stare could do to a man. "Some say," she continued, "that it was derived from the ancient Greek word *gamos,* meaning a '*marriage,*' or '*joining,*' as in a special kindred relationship between hunter and prey. And yes, when I hunt, Detective, that's my game. A relationship, an emotional connection with my quarry. It's the way things are done out here. We are all connected. And it's the same *game* Kurtz Steiger plays."

"What makes you think you know anything at all about this man?"

"Because I saw right there on that newscast that the Bush Man doesn't use humans for simple target practice. That would be too easy. He flushes them out, strips them down to their most basic, atavistic impulses, then he puts them on the run, chases them for days sometimes, toying with their minds, playing on their mental weaknesses. He needs them to *know* he is out there, watching them, hunting them with an expectation of kill. He wants this relationship, and he wants it up close and personal, because he feeds off the smell of human fear."

"And you think you're telling me something new?"

She was angering him, but she was not going to back down and concede defeat now. "Yeah, I do think so," she said. "It's a small matter of perspective, Sergeant. It makes a huge difference."

He exhaled angrily, dragging his hand over his hair. "Will you please just call me Gabe?"

Surprise rippled through Silver, and a smile tempted her lips. She almost gave in to it, but didn't. "You need to see the wilds differently before you can 'see' Steiger," she said. "Some of those law enforcement and military trackers might know how to cut from one footprint to the next, but the ones who can really 'see' know where to find their quarry without even looking, just from one track. Like an archaeologist can reconstruct an entire animal using a single bone, a good tracker can use one print to piece together an elaborate story of interlocking events. And that can lead him right to the source without taking a step."

"That's psychic bull." He leaned closer, his mouth coming near hers, and her blood warmed. A tiny warning bell began to clang in the back of Silver's brain, but she couldn't stand down. She stared him straight in the eye instead.

"And a woman like you shouldn't even begin to think of messing with a monster like Steiger." His voice was low, gravelly.

"Why? Because I'm female?" she asked softly.

"Because I've seen what that man does to women. You may be good, Silver, but you're not that good. You're no match for him. I *know* this."

"Maybe where you come from, Gabe, but out here, things are different. We know that the wolf, while strong, can still be outwitted by the hare."

Silver turned and walked away, her pulse racing much too fast, her palms clammy, her mouth dry. She hadn't meant to press him like that. God knew she should have let him be.

She was only making trouble for herself.

She sucked air in deeply, conscious once again of the tight ragged scar pulling across her chest—a reminder of just how carefully she needed to tread with Sergeant Gabriel Caruso.

He trekked down the hill toward Dawson City, late-morning mist shrouding the old gold rush boomtown that lay at the confluence of the Klondike and Yukon Rivers. It was almost three days since his escape, and his face had been plastered all over the news. He needed to be careful.

In the town's small library, he pulled the flaps of his fur-lined hunting cap down low, shading his profile as he began searching the Internet for information on Black Arrow Falls.

He'd taken the cap and some clothes from the small cabin by the river where he'd sewn up his leg. At a gas station a few miles out from the cabin, he'd crawled from the shadows and strapped himself under a logging rig. He'd heard the driver say he was heading north. He'd then liberated weapons from a hunting camp outside Whitehorse, busted into another remote cabin farther up the Klondike Highway, and found food and antiseptic for the leg wound still troubling him.

He'd cleaned up thoroughly each time, leaving no trace. He didn't want to telegraph his actions to Caruso.

He wanted to surprise him.

And he felt controlled, the steady, throbbing pain in his leg keeping him on a keen edge. Pain was his friend. Patience the art of the predator.

Scrolling through the Yukon newspaper online archives, his attention was instantly snared by a *Whitehorse Star* online report about Silver Karvonen, a tracker who'd located an eleven-year-old boy north of Whitehorse last month, after everyone else had given up hope. He leaned closer. The story said she possessed a tracking skill bordering on psychic. But it was what the next line said that made the blood in his groin grow hot—Silver Karvonen was from Black Arrow Falls.

He quickly punched her name into a search engine.

Almost immediately he came across several articles dating back five years—Karvonen had been a person of interest in an RCMP homicide investigation into the death of an Alaskan bootlegger named David Radkin.

That man had been the father of Karvonen's seven-year-old son, Johnny, who'd been found drowned and buried under a cairn of rocks near the remains of Radkin's body in remote bush northwest of Black Arrow Falls near an abandoned gold mine.

It appeared that a bear had been lured to the site by bloody rags hung from a tree. This had piqued police interest. The RCMP had questioned Silver but hadn't been able to prove anything. The bear had destroyed much of Radkin's body, along with any evidence.

It remained an unsolved mystery.

He leaned even closer, poring over the grainy black-and-white photograph of what was clearly a wild and beautiful woman.

He felt that familiar tingling thrill of anticipation begin to flood through his belly, that glorious rush into his blood. And Kurtz Steiger knew immediately what he wanted.

Whatever game he chose to play up in Black Arrow Falls, Silver Karvonen was going to be the centerpiece. Worthy prey. *A real hunt.*

He logged out of the library computer and sensed the librarian suddenly watching him intently.

He paused, thinking fast.

The library was quiet.

The only other librarian had stepped out earlier. There were three elderly patrons besides himself in the facility, and they sat hidden from sight at a big square table situated behind a row of shelves. Steiger slid his eyes slowly up and met the librarian's gaze squarely.

She swallowed.

He could see a quick flicker of recognition, yet there was also uncertainty in her eyes. She seemed unable to move, or to tear her gaze away from his riveting stare, mesmerized by some quality in him. He had that effect on people. He knew how to use it.

And he had maybe seconds before she reached for that phone sitting just inches from her hand.

Trapping her eyes with his, he scribbled something on a piece of paper, then surged smoothly to his feet, allowing a smile to curl over his lips as he approached her desk.

She looked up, terrified. "Can…I help you?"

He held out his hand, deepening his smile. "Could you tell me where this guide book is located?"

Confused, she dropped her gaze to his hand. Steiger used the instant to whip his hand to her shoulder, where he pressed down and dug his fingers down hard and fast into a pressure point at the base of her scrawny neck.

The librarian's eyes widened. Her mouth opened in a silent scream, and her body slumped. Steiger stepped quickly around the desk, lifting her small body up effortlessly, and he carried her out of the building as if helping a sick and fainting woman by bringing her into fresh air.

The library doors swung silently shut behind them.

The street was clear.

He ducked round the side of the wood structure, making for the nearby forest.

By the time they found her body, he thought, they'd

have nothing to connect her to him. He'd be long gone, his job long done.

Caruso would be long dead.

And so would that pretty tracker.

Chapter 5

Gabe had not seen Silver since their standoff in the bar two days earlier, and he found himself subconsciously looking for her as he went about the business of acquainting himself with the town.

She'd infuriated him with her criticism. It had cost him his soul to put that sick bastard behind bars, and there she was saying they'd done it wrong. That they could have had him sooner.

The unspoken implication being that Gia might have lived.

But even as Silver had laid raw his vulnerable spots, Gabe had gone home that night and lain awake on his wooden bed, one arm hooked under his head, watching the chunk of moon cross the Arctic sky. And instead of dwelling on Steiger, he found himself wondering how Silver might be in bed, how her smooth brown skin would feel under his fingertips, if she'd make love with the same fire that crackled in her laser-blue eyes. Gabe didn't know whether to be shocked with himself, or bemused, to even be thinking about sex—about living—again.

And even though he hadn't slept that night, he'd started the next day with an unexpected and welcome bite of energy.

Coming out of the band office, where he'd just set up a system for weekly briefings with Chief Peters, Gabe lowered his shades against harsh sunlight.

The band council had been leery of him. He was the new *cheechako,* as they called those from south of the sixtieth parallel, but sometime in the last two days Gabe had decided to knuckle down on his tenure, show them—one way or another—that he was here *for* them. And not against them.

He'd be lying to himself if he pretended Silver had not inspired him to do it.

Which is why he so badly, and so strangely, needed to see her again.

He told himself it was to talk about Steiger, and tracking. But in some weird way, Gabe realized he was seeking her approval. Lord knew he hadn't done anything right in anyone's eyes for some time now—especially his own.

A man could do with a little appreciation once in a while.

He squinted up at the jagged peaks to the northwest that marked the Alaskan border. From there, the granite mountains softened into foothills that rolled down toward Black Arrow Falls in the classic rounded hummocks of the Yukon's muskeg plains.

The Gwitchin of this region got their name from the Black Arrow River that ran down from those glaciers and fed into the Porcupine. The town itself was named for the falls, a small area where the river narrowed sharply, the land dropped, and water thundered over black rocks in a churning white froth.

Gabe studied the distant massifs. A dark cloud bank was building over them—a looming storm front.

That's when he saw a small red prop plane, flying errati-cally across the clouds before dipping and veering sharply left. He'd seen the same plane earlier, flying low just west of town. He frowned. It must be real gusty up there. He watched as the plane corrected, steadied, and began a rapid descent into the bush some miles north.

Wherever that plane was headed, Gabe reckoned it fell within the five thousand square miles he and his tiny detachment was now responsible for policing. He made a mental note to find out what was in that region as he hopped back onto his ATV and drove down to the lodge.

Silver wasn't there.

The lodge staff told him she was out hunting. They didn't know where, or when she'd be back. Could be days, maybe weeks.

Gabe glanced at the clouds again and felt edgy.

He told himself it was just the weather, the rapidly shortening hours of sunlight, the looming threat of a forbidding winter. But deep down he was worried about Silver.

Back in his office Gabe studied the topographical maps of the region. He and Donovan were working alternating shifts at the moment, so it was just him and Rosie in the detachment as he tried to pinpoint where the small plane could have gone down.

"Do you know what's in this area here, Rosie?" he asked, coming up to her desk with the map. He pointed to a long, narrow lake he figured the plane could use to touch down. It was several miles long.

"That's Wolverine Lake," she said. "And over there—" she pointed with her pen "—that's were the old Wolverine Gorge gold mine is. It was abandoned some years back when they discovered a massive geological fault in the rock wall that held back a small mountain lake. If blasting weakened that fissure, the whole lake could have busted through and flooded the tunnels, drowning the miners." She glanced up at him. "Why?"

"I saw a plane heading in for a landing in that direction."

"Good hunting up there," she said. "Probably a party taking one last crack at it before the season closes."

"Yeah. That's probably it."

He'd have to make a trip into that area next summer, Gabe thought, as he picked up his phone and punched in Tom's number, anxious for an update on the hunt for Steiger.

"Hey, buddy," he said as Tom answered his call. "Any word?"

"Not a damn thing. They're figuring Steiger tried to swim the river and went down in the floodwater."

"Drowned?"

"Everything points to that. The clothes and weapon he took from the warden have been found washed up in flood debris. Steiger was pretty badly injured as it was. He left a ton of blood in that prison van, and if he went into that flooded river in a weakened state, there was just no way in hell even he could have survived. They're dredging now. I'll call as soon as they find something."

Gabe hung up, leaned back in his chair, feeling oddly flat. Maybe the monster was human after all.

"Can you circle over that area down there?" Steiger spoke loudly into the headset so the pilot could hear him above the roar of the small, single-engine prop plane.

His beard was growing in, and his cheeks were gaunt. He wore his hat pulled low, and he looked different from the news photos. He carried himself differently, too, a feigned stoop hiding his power. His special ops training—which had taught him to blend into hostile environments—was serving him well.

The pilot banked sharply and buzzed low over a plateau. Steiger peered out the small, scratched window, studying the area carefully, memorizing topographical details. A lone teepee suddenly loomed into view. It stood in the middle of a clearing up high on the ridge, and an old man came out, waving a greeting as they flew over.

The pilot waved cheerily back. "That's Old Crow," he told his passenger, warm eyes twinkling as he shot a look at

Steiger. "He's a Black Arrow elder, a bit of a loner. Runs a couple of traplines in this area."

"You know the people of Black Arrow Falls?"

"Sure do," the pilot said. "I fly hunters in here a couple of times each summer, and I usually stay overnight in Black Arrow Falls before heading back to Dawson. Gives me some time away from the wife, if you know what I mean." He gave Steiger a conspiratorial grin. "They're real low-key, friendly folk in Black Arrow."

"So you'd know about the famous tracker, then, Karvonen?"

"Now *there's* a story. That old guy in the teepee down there is like her grandfather, taught her everything she knows. Why? You looking to use her as a guide? She's good, especially with the big game. Lots of my clients come up here just for her."

Steiger felt a hot zing of excitement. He moistened his lips. "I've read about her," he said quietly, studying the location of the teepee. "And I am interested in her skills. But I want to do some hunting up at Wolverine Gorge first. Alone. I might seek her out later." He shot the pilot the engaging smile of a true psychopath, his voice studiously warm.

"So when would you like me to fly in for pickup, then?"

Steiger fingered down the side of his leg, felt for the hunting knife at his calf, unsheathed it slowly. "I won't be needing pickup."

The pilot's eyes flared to his. "No pickup?"

"No. Just set me down on Wolverine Lake, the south end, real close to the mine."

"No can do. That wasn't our deal. I need to go in at the north end, which is several miles out from the mine. Won't be able to get this ol' Beaver back into the air again otherwise, given the direction of this wind."

"You won't need to."

Something in the tone of Steiger's voice stilled the pilot. He hesitated, hands tensing slowly on the controls. Suddenly he didn't want to meet his passenger's eyes, afraid of what he might find there.

Then the pilot felt the cold blade of a hunting knife press against his neck, and something in his heart sank like a cold stone.

"Now listen real carefully, buddy," his passenger said. "You radio in, cancel this flight plan, and you file another one to the south. Then you leave a message for that wife of yours. Tell her you're going to be gone another week. And then you set this puppy down, just like I said. North end of Wolverine Lake."

The deep end, where no one will see the plane wreckage under water.

Five days later Steiger was standing in the dark night, watching quietly through the cabin window as the young RCMP constable opened his fridge door and poured himself a glass of juice.

The cop was in his kitchen, out of uniform, his television flickering in the living room behind him. The man liked his juice. Steiger knew a lot about what the constable liked now. He'd been watching him for a full forty-eight hours.

He knew where the man put his gun and radio when he came home. He knew where he hung his uniform. He knew what time he put out his lights at night.

Steiger left the cover of trees and crept over to a dark shed behind the constable's cabin. Carefully, he creaked open the wooden door.

He was familiar with the lay of the entire town now. He knew where Sergeant Gabriel Caruso lived and worked. And he knew who he worked with. He knew where he bought his groceries and when his civilian assistant slipped out for lunch.

He'd also seen how the Black Arrow Falls telecommunications system functioned, and he'd worked out when the planes came in.

Flicking on the penlight he'd taken from the pilot's jacket he now wore, he panned the shed's interior. The cop's ATV was still warm, cans of gas on the shelf. His helmet and winter boots, too. And antifreeze.

He smiled as the game took shape in his mind.

The day dawned cold. By lunchtime, a sharp wind whipped through the streets, and Gabe could no longer see the mountains to the northwest. The black cloud had socked down, threatening to creep closer to town, and the barometer was dropping fast.

Constable Annie Lavalle had called earlier to say the White-horse court case was being delayed and so was her return to Black Arrow Falls. Constable Huong was still due another week of leave, and this morning, Donovan had called in sick.

Gabe was on his own.

He yanked up the collar of his uniform jacket and trudged across the deserted street to the general store. Although the sky was still clear over Black Arrow Falls, the low-pressure cell in the forecast was massive. The first winter snows were on their way.

And still no sign of Silver.

She'd been gone eight days now, and Gabe didn't like that she was still out there, alone, with this huge front closing in.

He told himself she'd been living up here for years, perfectly fine without his protection. It should be no different now. But he couldn't help himself.

Then just as he reached for the handle of the store door, his radio crackled.

Gabe frowned, glancing back across the street at the RCMP detachment. He keyed his radio. "What is it, Rosie? I can just about see you from here."

"It's Jake Onefeather, Sarge. He wants you to get down to the Old Moose lodge ASAP. He thinks there's a robbery."

"He thinks?"

"He was going to try and call Silver—he's worried about her with this weather coming in so fast. But he says the lodge satellite phones are missing."

Silver picked her way up a steep, rocky trail, ground falling sharply to her left in a ragged tumble of talus and scree, small stones skittering down into the ravine from under her feet as she moved with her dogs. A fat marmot watched her from atop a rock, fur ruffling silently in the wind.

She'd been out on the land for over a week now, and her head felt clear, her body strong and true. She loved the way being out in the wilderness both grounded and liberated her at the same time. Her mare, however, had stumbled in thick tussock yesterday, hurting her leg. Silver had been walking her ever since. It had slowed her down, but she wasn't worried—and there was no one to worry for her.

Abruptly, her dogs halted, hackles rising. Growls rolled deep in their chests. Valkoinen, her biggest, oldest white wolf cross, bared his incisors. Something was ahead of them on the trail. Something the dogs weren't familiar with.

Silver froze. Easing her rifle sling round, she clicked off the safety.

Wind rustled sharply through the tops of dry berry bushes, dead leaves clattering loudly against the branches of an alder, the sound reminiscent of rain. The wind carried the scent of old wood smoke, a fire gone cold.

A chill whispered over her skin.

She watched the ears on her dogs, the sensation of being watched herself making the hair on the back of her neck stand on end. Her heart began to thud softly.

She could feel a presence.

A predator.

She whispered for her dogs to heel. They came obediently to her side but remained edgy. She turned in a slow circle, gun leading, eyes carefully probing the vegetation, but she could see nothing unusual.

Silver continued up to Old Crow's camp, every sense alert, perspiration pricking over her skin in spite of the cool air.

Old Crow usually detected her approach from way back. He'd have his old black kettle swung out on the tripod over the fire, water boiling and ready for sweet black tea by the time she arrived.

But his tripod sat bare over a dead fire.

His blackened kettle lay overturned on the ground, a darker patch evident where the contents had spilled into earth. A loose piece of hide covering the entrance to his teepee flapped in the dry breeze.

Clap. Clap. Clap.

The chill down her spine intensified.

High above a golden eagle and a raven circled on air thermals, and Silver closed her eyes tight for a second, not wanting to read the signs.

She fingered her trigger, and called Old Crow's name out. Loud.

Her voiced echoed, bouncing back at her from the rock cliffs, the sound dying off into the valley.

But no reply came from Old Crow.

She moved toward his teepee.

Jake Onefeather pushed open the storeroom door. "The lodge sat phones are usually kept in here, on that top shelf. Someone's taken them all."

The only thing that rested on the shelf now was a solitary black feather that looked as though it had come from a crow, or a raven.

Gabe picked it up. It shimmered as he twirled it between his thumb and forefinger. He frowned, glanced at Jake. "How many phones were in here?"

"Three. I thought Silver might have taken one with her, and

I wanted to see which one so I could call her. This storm front is much bigger than we expected and moving in fast…" He shrugged. "I just thought I'd check on her."

Gabe raised a brow, vaguely comforted by the fact that he wasn't the only one concerned about a woman out hunting alone in some of the harshest wilderness around. "Does she usually take a sat phone with her on hunting trips?"

"Generally not, if she's without clients. She prefers the sense of freedom that comes with being out of reach, but I came down here to check on the off chance she had."

"And the door was locked, no sign of break-in?"

"No." Jake shifted his weight onto his other foot, clearly uneasy.

"Where do you keep the keys to this room?"

"On the key rack, near the bar, with the other lodge keys."

"*All* the lodge keys?"

"This is a safe place, Sarge."

Gabe took another look at the feather in his hand, wondering how it could have gotten in here, then he tucked it into his pocket. "Maybe Silver put the phones somewhere else, Jake," he said.

Jake's eyes narrowed. "She didn't. They were here."

"Okay, let's do this another way. Do you have the numbers for the missing phones?"

"Of course. I called them all but couldn't get through to anything from our landlines."

"Give me those numbers, and I'll head back to the detachment and try and call them from one of the RCMP sat phones, okay? If we're lucky, Silver will answer one of them and tell us where the other phones are."

"Sure, Sarge." But Jake Onefeather looked anything but. And for some reason, that rattled Gabe.

There'd been a scuffle—bare footprints and large boot tracks overlapped in the packed dirt in front of Old Crow's tent.

Panic strafed through Silver. She glanced over her shoulder, telling her dogs to stand guard as she crouched down to examine the dirt.

The boots were mukluks, about a men's size 12, hundreds of small distinctive round studs in the soles. Silver would know that pattern anywhere—they were RCMP winter issue.

A cop had been here?

Her head began to pound.

She peered closer. The bare feet belonged to Old Crow—he had a wide gap between his large toe and the rest of his toes, and a scar under his heel. She'd seen his feet often enough when she was a child, and they'd dangled their legs together in the river.

The boot tracks mostly lay atop the footprints, as if Old Crow had been shoved around in front of a powerful male. Then Silver saw what looked like naked knee imprints. And handprints, fingers splayed wide next to what might be small, dark spatters of blood. Old Crow had been hit, knocked to the ground where he fell hard to his knees, bracing with his hands, bleeding. Silver's eyes burned, and her heart clenched.

She glanced at her dogs, watching them for warning signs, and then she edged backward toward the teepee, gun trained on the surrounding bush.

She lifted the flap, entered the tent.

Old Crow's rifle lay on the ground.

He would never have left camp without it. Nor his weathered leather jacket, which lay in a crumpled pile alongside his weapon. His boots and pants, too.

Silver tried to swallow against the dread rising in her throat.

She walked out of the tent, showed her dogs the jacket. They sniffed, eager to be working, and she motioned for them to start finding scent. It would be faster than tracking the prints. She could take a closer look at the scuffle marks and tracks later, but right now she was hell-bent on finding Old Crow as quickly as she could.

They moved fast, her animals snuffling along a narrow trail through brush that led out from the back of the encampment. She could see the same foot- and bootprints along the trail, the mukluks atop the bare feet. Someone in cop boots had forced Old Crow along this trail in front of him, probably naked, judging by the clothes left in the teepee.

She felt sick.

Valkoinen froze suddenly, his tail dead straight—a sign that he'd sighted his quarry. A growl emanated from very low in his chest. Aumu and Lassi joined him, similar sounds issuing from deep in their throats. Warning sounds that curdled through Silver's gut, her sense of terror mounting as she edged forward.

She saw what had stopped her dogs. A loose mound of branches, earth, and other forest debris lay on the trail ahead.

A fresh kill site.

Grizzly.

Her stomach tightened so sharply she caught her breath.

Silver instantly reined her dogs back. Happening upon a fresh kill site was *always* a no-win situation. The bear could still be near, hidden in brush, ready to charge and kill in defense of his stashed prey. She needed to leave the area at once.

But she couldn't. Not until she learned what had happened to Old Crow.

Sweat dampened Silver's torso as she crouched down, carefully nudging back the debris with the barrel of her rifle.

It was him. Old Crow.

A buzz sounded inside her head. Her vision blurred.

Silver forced herself to stay focused, aware of the bush behind her.

Listening for the low cough of an angry grizz, she edged the debris back further, and bile surged into her throat. She struggled to swallow it down. The bear had started feeding on the soft stomach, leaving the head intact enough for Silver to see that her old mentor's throat had been cut. With a knife. Clean down to the spinal column. It wasn't a grizz that had killed him.

Old Crow had been murdered.

She glanced up sharply, scanning the surrounding vegetation, heart pounding.

Whispering to her dogs to keep watch, Silver edged away more of the debris, exposing Old Crow's hand. He was clutching something, his nails shredded and bloody. Silver tried to separate her mind from emotion as she leaned closer, to see what was in his fist. It was bits of hair. Pale ash blond. She tried to pry open his gnarled fingers, but he was going stiff with rigor. She managed to pull some of the strands out the side of his fist. Old Crow had fought hard. And he'd left her a clue.

"I'll get him," she whispered. "I'll get the bastard who did this."

Someone wearing RCMP boots had forced the one person in this world she cared most about along this trail, naked. Beaten him. And then slit his throat.

The bear must have come later, attracted by the scent of blood.

What monster could have done such a terrible thing. And *why?*

That's what scared her the most.

Silver quickly scanned the ground around the debris pile, her sense of urgency mounting.

What she saw confirmed that the bear had come later. Its massive prints lay atop the human ones. Then Silver saw the distinctive Broken Claw pattern, and her heart plummeted.

It was the sow she'd been tracking, the one who had mauled the hunter.

Silver was now wet with sweat.

The grizz would be back. And now she really *had* acquired a taste for human blood.

This was wrong. Everything felt off. She should leave at once, yet she was compelled to look further, a terrifying sense of déjà vu beginning to swamp her.

She whispered for her dogs to heel, and they began to follow the bear tracks down a barely discernable trail into a densely wooded area.

Nothing could have prepared Silver for what she saw next.

Hanging in the bare branches of a black cottonwood, flapping in the chill wind, were blood-soaked ribbons of rags, sending the scent of fresh meat into the hills.

That's what had drawn her bear.

Silver closed her eyes for a moment, trying to steady herself. This couldn't be real. This couldn't be happening.

Why would anyone do this? Was this a message for her? *Who could know?*

She tried to swallow, couldn't. She felt as though something were crushing her chest.

She needed to get Gabe up here. Fast. Before they lost light.

At the same time, she knew this would lead to questions. The parallels would lead the police directly to her, to the cold case she and the town would rather keep buried in RCMP files.

But Silver didn't have a choice.

Then she thought of the bootprints—*RCMP* boots. And her mind doubled in on itself, confusion and grief tormenting her, getting the better of her self-control.

Silver began to shake. She backed away very slowly, the sound of her own blood rushing in her ears, mesmerized by the fabric ribbons darkened with blood, flapping in the Arctic wind.

Chapter 6

Gabe headed back to the village trying to tell himself again that his uneasiness was probably just his body adjusting to the first looming storm of winter. Both pressure and temperature had been falling steadily since he'd arrived, each day bringing noticeably less daylight. That had to affect a person's body.

Rosie glanced up as he entered the detachment, her smile dimpling her round cheeks, and Gabe warmed.

"Hey, Sarge."

"That my new official tag up here, eh, Rosie?" he asked with a smile of his own. And yes, it did feel good. To smile. It eased the anxiety tightening inexplicably in his chest.

Gabe went straight to get a sat phone from the equipment room. But as he inserted the key, he found the door unlocked. Puzzled, he pushed open the door, and froze.

The RCMP phones were gone.

"Rosie!"

She came bustling along the passage, drawing her sweater over her shoulders. "What is it, Sarge?"

"Did Donovan take the satellite phones?"

"I…I don't know. He would have signed them out if he had."

Gabe grabbed the signout sheet. It was blank.

Tension balled in his stomach. "Who else came into the detachment today? Why isn't this door locked? It's an evidence room, dammit. We have weapons in here."

Rosie faltered. "I…I don't know. I…I don't handle the room. That's the officers' business. Donovan has a key in his drawer, I think."

"Who else has a key?"

"No one, sir. I mean, you do, sir."

Her dark brown eyes were watering and Gabe cursed himself for taking it out on a civilian. His rage was flaring too quickly again. He placed his hand on her shoulder. "Hey, I'm sorry, Rosie," he said, softening his tone as he led her back to her desk.

He sat opposite her. "It's just that having that door open is serious. There are weapons in there. Evidence. Court cases could be lost if protocol is compromised. I want you to think, Rosie. Did anyone come by the detachment today?"

"Yes, but…but they didn't get past the reception area."

"*Who* stopped by, Rosie?"

She moistened her lips. "A few people. Henry Two Rivers— he came to say hello. Eddie Linklater wanted to file a complaint against Joey Kyikavichik, and Joey wanted to file one against Eddie in return. They do that all the time. I told them—"

"Did you leave the reception desk at any time?"

"I went to the washroom. But it was real quick. I don't think anyone could have come round. We've…" her voice hitched. "I've never had a problem with the other officers before."

"You didn't leave the building at any time?"

She flushed. "I…I just ran across the road to Edith's store for a soup at lunch. I came straight back. I was hardly gone a minute."

He sucked in air slowly, very slowly. "Do you go to Edith's for lunch often, Rosie?"

She nodded, casting her eyes down. "Most days. I call ahead with my order."

"So it's a routine, something someone could pick up if they were watching the detachment and wanted to get in and take the phones for some reason?"

She looked up, horrified. "Who would do such a—"

"Rosie." He leaned forward. "Did you do this soup thing over the past four or five days?"

She nodded.

Gabe swore to himself. He was going to have to make some serious changes to detachment security.

In the meantime, he had to find out what in hell happened to those RCMP phones, and check against the logs to see what else was missing. He thought of the Old Moose Lodge, the empty shelf in the storage shed. The black feather in his pocket.

But as he stood up from Rosie's desk, the detachment door banged open, and both Gabe and Rosie jerked round in shock.

Silver stood against the sunlight, a shotgun clenched in her hand, her face pale, eyes strangely wild. There was blood on her sleeve.

Gabe's pulse cracked up a notch.

He stood slowly, hand moving reflexively to his sidearm. "Rosie," he said quietly, attention trained on Silver's eyes and the pump action twelve-gauge in her hand. "Why don't you step outside for a moment." He kept his tone calm, yet brooking no resistance.

Rosie quickly gathered her sweater over her shoulders and left, the screen door slapping gently into place behind her.

"Silver?" He held out his hand. "Why don't you give me that gun?"

Her gaze swept over him, settling briefly on his boots, as if computing the size. She glanced around the station, edgy. "Where's Donovan?"

"The gun, Silver. Please?"

She let him take it.

Gabe noticed that her hands were trembling. He pointed the barrel of her Winchester away from them, checked to see that the safety was on, depressed the action release and repeatedly pumped until all the rounds were ejected, then set the gun down.

"Donovan's home sick," he said. "Now why don't you talk to me?"

Her dark brows lowered fiercely. "The other cops—are they both still out of town?"

"Silver, what is this about?"

"Old Crow has been murdered." Her voice was rough, as if she'd been running, or riding hard. "Up on the plateau. You need to come. Now. Before we lose light." She drew a sheaf of folded tissue paper from her pocket as she spoke. She held it out to him, eyes glittering like hard blue diamonds.

"What is this?" Gabe said, looking at the tissue.

"That's who killed him."

He unfolded the tissue slowly, tension winding tight inside him.

A few short strands of dead-straight hair rested on the paper, very pale ash blond. Cold knifed down his spine as Gabe stared at the hair. "Where did you get this?"

"It was clutched in Old Crow's hand," she said. "Rigor was just setting in. He'd been dead maybe two hours before I found him. The killer has short pale hair, is about six-foot-two, 180 pounds. Very strong. Very fit."

His eyes shot to her. "You *saw* him?"

"I didn't need to. That's what his tracks told me."

It couldn't be. Not Steiger.

Gabe tried to shut the insane thought out but it hammered its way in and bounced around his skull. He grabbed the ATV keys. "Show me!"

"You aren't getting in there on a quad, Sergeant. I have

fresh horses waiting," she said. "And you'd better bring a camera, because the evidence isn't going to stay there long." Silver hesitated. "There's…wildlife."

Silver slid her eyes over to Gabe as they rode silently side by side. He looked at home on that mount in his uniform. Damn good, in fact. He was solid. Real. Strong.

And she felt oddly abandoned. Hollow. As if her insides had been scooped out. She tried not to think about Old Crow, the fact that his absence would leave a permanent hole in her life. He was the closest thing she had to family.

She'd known he would leave some day. But not like this.

"Gabe?" she said.

He turned his head, warm brown eyes meeting hers, and her heart did that silly little involuntary tumble again. She tightened her grip on the reins. "When you saw the hair, you…" she hesitated. "You looked as though you recognized something."

His mouth tightened. "It was nothing," he said.

She held his eyes. "I don't believe you."

"I need to see the scene, Silver," he said. "I need to be sure it's a homicide."

She glanced away. He knew something and was hiding it from her. It made her feel even more uneasy.

They rode in silence a few moments longer, but she could feel him watching her. "The satellite phones for the Old Moose Lodge," he said suddenly. "Did you move them?"

Her eyes whipped to his. "What?"

"They're missing from the storage room."

She reined her horse to a sharp stop. "What the hell were you doing in *my* storeroom?"

"Jake called me in. He thinks the phones were stolen. I suggested you might simply have put them somewhere else."

Her eyes narrowed sharply. "I didn't."

"And you didn't take one with you?"

"No. Why was Jake looking for the phones, anyway? They're for the hunting parties. And we're closed for the season."

"He was worried about you with this storm coming. So was I."

Her mouth opened. She shut it quickly. Unexpected and conflicting emotions twisted through Silver—mistrust, a spurt of affection, confusion—she settled on anger, the easiest to deal with. "What the hell were you worried for?"

"I'm not used to a woman going off hunting for—"

"Well, get used to it!" She spun her horse round, kicked it forward into a gallop, tension whipping around her heart.

It was a mistake to involve herself with Gabe Caruso. But she had no choice.

Right now he was the only cop in town.

They dismounted in silence, entering the encampment on foot.

Apart from a loose piece of hide slapping against the tent in the wind, it was eerily silent. Desolate.

Silver held her pump-action shotgun ready at her side, clearly not taking chances with a rifle.

Gabe took in the big teepee, the cooking area in front, the tripod over blackened logs, the overturned pot.

Tension coiled in his gut.

Silver whispered for her dogs to stand guard while Gabe took photographs of the approach. He was acutely conscious of sound. Or the lack of it.

"Where's the body?" he said, moving into the camp.

She placed a hand on his arm, stopping him from treading on tracks. "You need to see these first." She crouched down, motioning him to do the same.

As he did, he caught the soft lavender scent of her hair, felt her skin brush his, and instinctively his stomach tightened and warmed. Damn odd time to feel that, he thought.

But she felt it, too—he could tell. Her eyes caught his, held for a long moment. Then her cheeks flushed suddenly, and she cast her eyes down. "The ground here is damp," she said quickly. "So these prints are really clear." She picked up a small stick, pointing to the depressions in the soil. Gabe leaned forward, his body brushing against hers again. A loud crack resounded nearby, and abruptly the bush went dead quiet.

Gabe's muscles compressed.

He glanced up, caught Silver's eyes. She was watching her dogs. Their teeth were bared, hackles rising, but they remained silent. "Something's out there," she whispered. "I felt it earlier, like someone was watching me. Everything in the bush went quiet. It felt almost…evil."

Gabe was uncannily edgy now that she'd voiced the same feelings. It *wasn't* just him. It was real.

"Stay close to me," he said softly.

"No. You stay close to me, Sergeant," she said, releasing the safety on her gun. "It could be the grizz coming back."

Tension shimmered over Gabe. He felt exposed crouching down in the soil like this. Like prey.

"We need to move faster," she said, eyeing her dogs. "See all these little round dents?" she pointed to the prints with her stick. "These tracks were made by RCMP mukluks. A men's size 12."

"What?"

Gabe glanced reflexively at his own operational footwear—hiking-style lace-to-toe ankle boots, good for most fall, winter and wet spring conditions, but no match for extreme Yukon winters. For those the RCMP issued dark-blue nylon-and-rubber outer shell arctic mukluks with a double wool inner liner. He swatted away a cloud of tiny black insects. "What on earth makes you think those are RCMP?"

She shot him a look, her darkly fringed eyes catching the gray light. It made them an eerie blue, like the eyes of her husky-wolf crosses. "I watch people, Sergeant. My town has a population of 389, and not all of them are adults, or men. I know their prints. I know their shoes. You have to trust me on this."

He studied her haunting blue eyes for a moment. He wasn't sure of anything with this unusual woman.

"Mukluks are winter issue," he said. "Neither Donovan nor myself have cracked those out yet. And there are no other cops in town."

"Well, these boots didn't belong to whoever left these tracks. See the wear pattern on the sole here?" she pointed at a print with her stick. "It indicates that the owner of these mukluks pronates badly—his feet turn outward when he walks so that the inner edge of his sole bears the weight of his body."

"So he walks a bit like a duck?"

"Yes, a bit like a duck," Silver said. "And you'd expect that gait to show in the position of these footprints. You'd also expect the pronation to show in soil depth on the insides of these prints. It doesn't. These are completely different. Whoever was wearing these mukluks has an easy, powerful roll onto the balls of his feet. A completely different stride."

Gabe rubbed his brow. "So someone stole cop boots? What for?"

"To mislead the police maybe?" she said, watching him intently. "Or…maybe to try and tell you something."

Cold slicked into Gabe's veins. He thought of the hair on the tissue. Silver's description of height and weight.

It *couldn't* be Kurtz. He refused to believe it.

And even if it was, where would he get RCMP boots?

Gabe thought of Donovan, sick and home alone. He thought of his constable's quirky stride, the way his feet turned outward. Donovan was about a size 12. The young constable had also worked several years in the North, enough time for the soles of his mukluks to show characteristic wear.

Gabe thought of Steiger's powerful, easy stride. He moved like an athlete.

He got to his feet, glancing at the bush, hyperaware of the rifle in his hand, the way his heart was thudding against his ribcage.

Silver touched his arm, and he just about jumped out of his skin. "The body is over this way," she said softly.

She led him past the teepee, showing him Old Crow's bare footprints, the depressions where the old man had stumbled onto hands and knees, the faint splatters of blood indicating he'd been struck along the way.

"He was naked?"

She nodded, mouth tight.

Gabe had seen this before.

The hikers Steiger had slain north of Jasper had been stripped naked and set on the run in the woods. Steiger had given them several hours' lead time, and then hunted the couple down easily. The stripping was a power ploy. A little game he liked to play.

He liked to pick on couples, too. He'd play on emotions, see how far a man could be pushed to save his woman. And then he'd rape the woman in front of the man, make him feel powerless while Steiger tortured and killed the woman he loved.

Gabe tried to imagine Old Crow, forced naked from his tent, being pistol-whipped down the trail, and his stomach steeled.

He didn't want to believe this could be the work of the Bush Man.

After all, Tom had said all evidence pointed to the fact that he'd drowned. Gabe was just haunted by memories. Consumed by his own rage. He needed to stay focused, or he was going to miss something vital here.

Yet the dark and murky whisperings in his soul wouldn't be quelled.

Then he saw them.

Three black feathers poking out from a small rock along the edge of the trail.

Gabe froze, stared at the feathers, feeling oddly hot and cold at the same time.

Clap. Clap. Clap.

The desolate sound of the loose piece of cowhide slapping against the tent as the wind gusted, unnerved him further

"What are those?" He pointed at the feathers with his rifle, his voice hoarse.

Silver looked at him, frowned. "Raven feathers," she said. "They're common. The birds molt."

He crouched down, picked one up, stared at it.

"Gabe," she said softly. "What is it?"

He swallowed. Should he tell her about the raven feather in her storeroom? That the RCMP phones were missing, too?

She was a civilian; he was a cop. This was a homicide. Yet the rules didn't seem to apply out here. Nothing applied. And damned if she wasn't the closest thing he had to a CSI right now—wild style.

He took the other feather from his pocket. "I found this in your storage shed, where the lodge phones should have been."

She took the feathers from him, her frown deepening as she compared them.

"These feathers were all plucked," she said. "Ripped from the bird. They're not normal molt, Gabe, their basal sheaths are still attached."

He got to his feet, heart pounding harder. "Which means?"

"It could be a sign of predation. And it wouldn't be unusual to find feathers torn from the flesh of a bird out here. But…"

"But it would be unusual to find one inside your storeroom?"

She stared at him, something strange and unreadable shifting into her eyes as she nodded.

Ice curdled through his veins, his mind battling to accept what the signs were telling him.

He thought of the small red prop plane flying erratically against the ragged ridge of granite.

If Kurtz Steiger had come to Black Arrow Falls, it could mean only one thing. He'd come for Gabe.

He'd come to finish the job.

And if he'd killed Old Crow, it meant Silver was now emotionally involved, too. Had that been Steiger's intention, to involve the tracker, a talented hunter herself?

Gabe thought of the complex and sadistic mind games Steiger liked to play, the challenges he set for himself, of how he enjoyed toying with couples in particular. Of how he'd taken such pleasure in hurting Gia and then letting Gabe know it.

Did he want to see Gabe fail in protecting another woman? Were he and Silver to be part of some sick new game?

If Steiger knew about Silver's connection to Old Crow, it meant he could have been watching her already. Like he'd been watching him and Gia in Williams Lake.

Gabe cursed under his breath.

If Silver was in Steiger's crosshairs, it was his fault.

He'd brought this evil to Black Arrow Falls.

Gabe's mouth flattened. "Show me the body, Silver." His voice was tight. He wanted to get her the hell out of here. As soon as possible.

Chapter 7

Silver lifted away the branches she'd replaced over the body of her old mentor, and Gabe's stomach twisted at the sight of mauled flesh.

He shot a glance at Silver.

Her body was tense, her features tight. She glared at him, right into his eyes, and he could sense her angry energy, the shimmering edge of violence. This was a woman who didn't get sad—she got mad.

Gabe knew just how much energy it took to hide pain behind that kind of rage. He'd been doing it for over a year.

An urge to gather her into his arms, hold her tight, swelled sharp and bittersweet in his chest. He needed to connect on some basic level, to let her know that he understood—more than she could ever imagine. Before he could rationalize, he cupped the side of her face firmly, holding her steady, her skin velvet and cool under his palm. "I'm sorry," he said. "I'm so sorry, Silver."

She swallowed, moving from his touch, lowering her eyes quickly. "See there?" She pointed to the clean, sharp slash on the victim's neck. Her gaze lifted slowly back to meet his. "Grizzlies don't use knives, Sergeant."

But Kurtz Steiger did.

"The hair," she said quietly, "was clutched in this hand here. Old Crow wanted to leave us a clue. He…he knew I would look, find it."

Or Steiger knew.

If this was the work of the Bush Man, every clue would have been left by design. From the police-issue bootprints, to the hair, the ripped raven feathers left as a calling card—these were the sorts of games Steiger played. The way he loved to taunt the police. It matched his profile to a T.

It was getting dark, the sky turning gunmetal gray, and the air growing cold. Gabe took his flashlight from his gun belt, directed the beam at Old Crow's fist, now held in rigor's death grip.

The elder's hands were wrinkled and tough, nails shredded and bloodied. He'd put up a valiant fight for his life.

Gabe clicked his camera, the flash momentarily throwing the mauled body into grotesque relief.

The method of homicide was also classic Steiger.

The Bush Man liked to reduce a man to his basest instincts. He believed if you cornered a victim, took everything away from him, that's when the animal would emerge. That's what gave Steiger power, a sadistic thrill. He needed to strip the humanity away, layer by layer, first. And taking the victim's clothes was just one way he achieved this. Gabe swore softly.

"I need to get a forensics team up here," he said, thinking of the missing sat phones, and how he could use one now. Memories of how he'd been isolated from help at Williams Lake suddenly felt like a noose around his neck. "We could have a team in from Whitehorse by first light," he said. "If I can radio Donovan on our way back and I can get him to call this in."

"There isn't going to be anything left of Old Crow by morning, Gabe," she whispered. "That grizz will be back. So will the rest of the scavenger guild. The foxes, coyotes, wolverines—they'll take what's left tonight. Nature's recyclers. That's why I needed you to come right away."

Gabe stilled as the beam of his flashlight illuminated a huge pawprint in the dirt alongside the burial mound. "Is that from the grizzly who did this?"

"That's the front left foot of the sow I was tracking earlier. See the broken claw mark?"

He shot her a look. "The one that attacked the hunter?"

Her eyes narrowed. "She's not a man killer, Gabe. This is not her fault. You saw that knife wound. *That's* what killed Old Crow. The bear came afterwards. See the way her prints are atop the human tracks? Over there, too."

He directed his flashlight to where she pointed. She was right.

"We need to find a way to transport him, then," he said. "We need to preserve what we can of this evidence."

She wavered, a haunted—almost frightened—look creeping into her eyes. It sent another surge of foreboding through him, and his pulse quickened.

"What is it, Silver?"

"I…need to show you something else. Down that track there." She nodded toward a barely discernable path that burrowed into dense scrub.

"Why? What's down there?"

She swallowed. "I…you…need to see it."

She led the way with her own flashlight.

Gabe exhaled slowly, trying to control his impulses as he followed her into the thicket. The trail was too narrow for his comfort, the vegetation too dense, too close. He felt like a rat being led into a maze. Like easy prey. His heart thudded in spite of his efforts to stay calm.

She led him about a hundred yards in, but she kept

glancing at her dogs as she went, edgy herself. Nerves bit deeper into Gabe.

The trail suddenly opened out into a small clearing.

"Up there." She aimed her flashlight into the twisted black branches of a leafless tree.

Ribbons of dark, torn, fabric flapped in the wind like some bizarre Halloween scarecrow.

"What the—"

"Blood lure," she said. "The killer soaked strips of Old Crow's shirt in his blood to attract wildlife," she said. "To cover his crime."

"No," Gabe whispered staring at the macabre strips of fabric. "He wouldn't do that. He wouldn't want to hide the evidence."

Her eyes whipped to his. "*Who* wouldn't do that? What are you talking about?"

"Unless…it's part of a puzzle," he whispered. "Part of the game."

"Gabe!" Her voice was angry, tense. "Dammit, what *are* you talking about?

A dark fear overtook him. There was absolutely no doubt in his mind now. Kurtz Steiger was here. *He'd* committed this murder. And a DNA test on those strands of hair would prove it.

He spun round, sweat breaking out over his body. They needed to get the hell off this plateau, before it got too dark.

"We need to leave, Silver. Now."

"Gabe!" She demanded. "Tell me—"

But before she could finish, they heard it—a sharp crack followed by a heavy crunch of vegetation. And a low, harsh cough.

Gabe jerked backward, adrenaline slamming into his blood, every hair on his body standing on end. He whipped his rifle stock to his shoulder, spun to face the sound, finger against trigger. Blood boomed in his ears.

Silver's dogs growled.

In one fluid movement she'd shouldered her shotgun and was aiming at the sound. She whispered for her dogs to heel, then she tapped Gabe gently on the arm, made a motion with her eyes for him to start backing away behind her.

Not on your life. He was supposed to protect her.

He narrowed his eyes angrily, flicked them to the side, telling *her* to get behind *him*.

"No," she hissed. "Start moving. Now!" But before he could react, a massive creature reared up out of the dense thicket on hind legs.

It was the grizz, back for her food stash.

She was about fifty yards away, mouth open, tasting their scent as she swayed her head from side to side, popping her jaws with a coughing sound.

Silver quietly ordered her dogs to stand still. Gabe could feel one of them near his leg, quivering to attack.

The bear dropped suddenly to the ground, eyes fixed dead on them, ears flat, saliva glistening. A low reverberating hum emanated from deep in her chest, and she advanced a few feet, front legs stiff, before swatting the ground hard with her paw. Gabe could smell the animal's hot breath, the powerful stench of carrion in her teeth.

Silver's dogs growled throatily. Again, she ordered them to hold back. They obeyed, holding their ground, eyes locked on the grizz. They were in a tense standoff now—one wrong move could bring instant death.

"Stay very quiet," she whispered to Gabe. "Back off behind me, at an angle."

"No way in hell. You go," he whispered at her.

"Dammit, this is no time to go chauvinist on me, Caruso," she hissed, eyes trained on the bear. *"Get the hell behind me!"*

Instead he sighted down the barrel, subtly increasing pressure on the trigger of his rifle.

"You pull that trigger, Gabe," she whispered angrily, "and we'll be dead before your bullet even registers."

He hesitated.

Silver was right. Unless he hit just right, his rifle wasn't going to stop five hundred pounds of enraged grizzly from barreling at them through dense brush at forty feet per second. Silver had a better chance with her shotgun slug.

"Don't shoot," she hissed. "If she does charge, stand your ground. No matter what, don't run. Now try and back away. Slowly. Maintain eye contact with her at all times."

"I thought that was a threat," he whispered.

"We're beyond that. Now go."

Gabe took two tentative steps back.

The bear immediately lowered her head and charged.

Every molecule in Gabe's body screamed to run, to shoot, to do something other than stand there like a giant sweating target in front of five hundred pounds of barreling fur-covered bone, muscle, and teeth. Time lengthened, and he thought this was it. This was where he died.

And suddenly, so goddamn sharply, he realized he didn't want to. He may have been looking to put himself in harm's way before he came north, but now that it was down to the wire, he wasn't ready to clock out.

Gabe's eyes narrowed onto the grizz, onto her small eyes and gleaming teeth. Blood boomed in his ears, and his heart pumped in his windpipe. Then at the last minute, the bear veered sharply to the left.

His stomach almost bottomed out. His torso was damp.

But it wasn't over. The bruin whirled round, faced them again, huffing, her hot breath crystallizing white in the cool evening. She swatted the ground, claws raking through dirt as she swayed her head from side to side, saliva dripping from her jowls.

God, they needed to get out of here—she was gearing up for another run at them.

But Silver remained motionless at his side. "Start backing, again," she whispered, shotgun aimed at the bear. "Nice and slow, not like you're scared, not like you're running away. Just let her know you don't want her stash, that you're not a threat—that's all she's worried about. Do not turn your back, Gabe. Don't run. It'll trigger chase. She'll kill you."

Gabe moved slightly, and immediately the bear charged again, coming so close to them this time that she almost knocked the barrel of Silver's gun as she peeled back at the last minute, fur rippling gold over her haunches. Silver held fast, didn't fire.

The sow repeated her aggressive ground slapping and huffing.

"Keep backing away," Silver whispered. "She's mad as hell. I...I don't know if we're going to get away from this one without engaging with her."

Great.

This time Gabe readied to fire.

He aimed for the front of the bear's shoulder, hoping to break her shoulder blade with his first shot, thus crippling her midcharge. His next bullet would be targeted to her chest. He made mental note of where his knife was strapped to his duty belt for last resort hand-to-claw combat, and his muscles compacted in anticipation of the fight as another surge of adrenaline rushed through him.

The bear dropped her head and charged again. Gabe's throat turned bone-dry. He began to pull the trigger, knowing instinctively that his bullet would never stop this bear now.

Chapter 8

Silver rammed her elbow against the barrel of Gabe's rifle, forcing his shot wide as she fired her own warning slug. It exploded into the packed dirt right in front of the animal, sand kicking sharply up into the grizzly's face. The bear hesitated, but then reared up, shaking her head aggressively, an unearthly moan reverberating in her chest, her mouth foaming with saliva.

Gabe swore violently at Silver. "What in hell do you think you're doing?"

"You nearly got us killed, dammit!" she hissed. "Don't ever do that to me again. I am your guide out here, understand? You obey *my* orders." Perspiration dampened Silver's chest as she stared the bear down.

Sometimes a warning shot worked. Other times it just infuriated them. Like now.

A bear was not a machine. There was no proscribed action for an encounter. Each attack had to be played from the gut and heart. She continued to lock eyes with Broken Claw, her finger light on the trigger of her twelve-gauge, her mind racing.

She told herself that she understood this bear. Broken Claw was stressed, afraid, but not predatory. She was just warning them to back off. But the smallest move in any direction now might trigger a final chase.

She had to risk it. Take the gamble. But it wasn't just her life. It was Gabe's, too.

The responsibility felt enormous.

Silver swallowed. "We've distracted her," she lied. "But we've got to act now. Start backing."

To his credit, this time Gabe obeyed instantly, but Silver could sense he was ready to shoot again if things went awry. He wasn't a coward. She knew plenty of hunters, big macho corporate leaders, who'd wet their pants rather than stand stock-still in the face of a full-on grizzly charge. And deep down she was totally taken by the way he'd tried to protect her, even though his misguided chivalry could have gotten them *both* killed.

Silver couldn't remember when someone last had fought to come to her rescue. She'd always had to be there for herself.

Yet Gabe was being man enough now to let her handle this her way.

And she didn't want to let him down.

That point could be moot, however, if Broken Claw charged for real this time.

Silver whispered to her dogs, ordering them to retreat down the trail ahead of her and Gabe. As her hounds moved obediently away, Silver and Gabe began backing away. Immediately the bear advanced again but more slowly this time.

She was allowing them to increase distance, opting to stay closer to her burial pile on the other side of the dense thicket.

They rounded a small bend, backing away faster as soon as they were out of the bear's line of sight. "Watch your feet," Silver whispered. "Trip on a root, and you're dead, Sergeant."

The bear rounded the bend after them and did a small mock charge before wheeling off abruptly and lumbering with crashing noises back through the brush toward her kill pile.

Silver exhaled shakily. "We're out of her bubble zone," she whispered. "But keep moving. Slow and steady. Just to be safe."

They entered the encampment, and Gabe slowly lowered his rifle, sweat beading across his forehead, glistening at the hollow of his neck.

"Bubble zone?" he said.

"A distance in which she feels safe. Every bear has one, and each distance is different. Breach that zone, and the bear responds as if threatened."

Same with humans.

Gabe's eyes bored into her. Exhilarated. A little wild. His pulse thrummed fast and hard at his neck. But he remained still, staring at her intensely in the fading light.

And right at that moment Silver wasn't sure where her own safety zone lay.

"You...okay?" she asked.

"Yeah," he whispered. "Oh, hell, yeah." He cupped her jaw, lifted it brusquely, kissed her hard and fast on the mouth.

Silver froze under him.

She could feel the thud of his heart against her breasts. He was hot, his whole body pumped. He felt so damn alive. Every molecule in her body reacted to his energy, coupling with it, beginning to hum with an electrical current that shocked her.

He pulled back, eyes animated.

"Thank you," he whispered. "You saved my ass back there."

Her own heart was now slamming so hard against her ribcage she couldn't breathe. Or hear. Her mouth was dry. Her mind numb. Her skin hot. She was conscious that danger still lurked close by, and somewhere in her brain she knew they still had to move. But he'd rocked something fundamental in her, and it was as though she didn't even know how to walk anymore.

Silver glanced toward the bush. Old Crow's body was in there, with the bear. And she was standing here, more alive than she'd ever felt in her life. With this man. But in some ways he represented an even bigger danger to her than the bear.

She felt far more in control staring down a charging grizzly at close range. She didn't know how to defend herself against Gabe. She didn't even know if she wanted to.

She began to tremble as the aftereffects of his kiss and her adrenaline took control.

"You're shaking," he said, touching her arm.

She nodded, emotion pushing against her eyes as she struggled to regain command over herself.

He smiled gently, his eyes softening. "So you are a mere mortal after all."

A nervous laugh escaped her, and he put his arm around her shoulders, leading her through the camp, back toward the horses, making sure she didn't look at Old Crow's teepee. "You challenged my pride back there, you know?"

He was trying to distract her, and she was thankful for it.

"And you questioned my authority, Gabe," she said, pulling herself together as she untied the horses. She handed him the reins.

"I didn't hire you, Silver," he said quietly. "I'm not your client, I'm a cop doing my job."

"And I know the rules out here. You don't. Next time you do something like that, Sergeant, you're going to get us *both* killed."

His eyes held hers, his features turning grave as he took the reins. "You going to be okay?"

She nodded, swung up into the saddle.

But by the way she refused to meet his eyes, Gabe knew she was anything but.

* * *

They rode in silence, carefully picking their way back down the rocky escarpment path, a gibbous moon rising to light their way. Stars spattered across an indigo-black sky, and a soft shimmer of northern lights billowed in gentle waves over the northern horizon, but to the west the sky was blotted out. The ominous black mass of cloud was growing bigger, roiling down over the hidden massifs and creeping along the foothills toward Black Arrow Falls, swallowing stars as it neared—a reminder of the imminent threat of winter.

It was unspeakably beautiful, though. Utterly silent. Harsh and unforgiving. The sheer scope of this landscape commanded respect, reverence even. It made Gabe feel part of something much bigger. It showed him that he was not necessarily at the top of the food chain out here, and that tended to shift a man's perspective.

He glanced at Silver on her horse. She was an enigma. Like this place. She, too, had challenged his conventions. And he wasn't sure how to handle her, either.

He hadn't been entirely truthful. It wasn't his ass he was thankful for her having saved back there. It was the fact that she'd shown him he still had the bite for life. That he didn't want to check out without one hell of a fight, because there was a lot more he still wanted to experience. Like the taste of her incredible mouth again.

He hadn't even thought twice before kissing her. And he wasn't sorry he had. He just didn't know where it would go from here.

But that mystery in itself, that promise of something more, shimmered inside him with the same magical electric energy as the aurora borealis along the horizon.

In some ways, Gabe realized, he'd had to come to the edge of nowhere before he could even begin to see that there *was* a road back.

But his coming north had also potentially put Silver in

danger. It had cost the life of someone precious to her, and he was obligated to her now, his life intertwining inextricably with hers, because of Steiger.

His chest tightened at the thought.

As they got closer to town, Gabe reached for his radio and keyed it. He needed to raise Donovan, get him to use his landline to call in the homicide and ERT guys from White-horse.

"Black Arrow, do you copy?"

Static crackled, whooshed.

"Black Arrow, can you read me?"

More white noise, static.

"Donovan? Are you there, Constable? Can you copy?"

The static hushed suddenly, as if someone had keyed to respond. Gabe tensed, waiting, finger poised over the key.

But there was only peculiar silence. As if someone were just listening.

Worry wormed into Gabe.

"Constable," he repeated. "Are you okay? Do you copy?"

Nothing.

He cursed softly.

"Maybe you're not in range of the repeater yet," Silver said, watching him.

"Yeah, that's probably it." But he felt his hands tighten on the reins. He *was* in range—he was certain of it—and he had the eeriest sensation that his transmission was being received and listened to.

But no one was answering.

Instinctively, he rode closer to Silver, coming up alongside her as the trail widened out onto the rolling muskeg and tussock plains. They were sitting targets in the moonlight. But they could also see for miles, and her dogs were watchful as they scampered along the trail, two ahead of the horses, one behind, white coats ghostly in the night.

The irony wasn't lost on him. He, the Mountie, was

relying on his guide and her dogs to alert him to a danger *he'd* brought into town.

"What kind of dogs are those?" he asked, trying to shake the eerie mood.

"Mongrels. Like me." She glanced at him. "Part wolf, part husky, part Karelian bear dog."

"The restraint they showed with that grizz was phenomenal."

"I trust them with my life. And they trust me."

Gabe didn't doubt they'd kill for her. "Karelian—that's a breed from northern Finland?"

She nodded. "Same region my dad came from. The province of Karelia straddled what is now the border of Finland and Russia. The Karelians were peasant dogs. The dogs of hunters. My father brought a pair with him when he came out here," she said. "He used to refer to the Karelian dog as a piece of untamed wilderness."

Gabe studied her striking profile on the horse, silhouetted against the dark rolling plains turning silvery with frost. She carried a rugged legacy, and he suspected that Silver had received an eclectic education unlike most. She was like this place. She embodied the spirit and strength of it. The wildness.

He also suspected that with Old Crow dead, she was also very much alone now, even though she had her Black Arrow clan and her dogs.

"How long has your father been gone, Silver?" he asked gently.

Her eyes whipped to his, suddenly glittering angry. "And just how long are you going to keep this up, Sergeant? When are you going to tell me what you were talking about back there, when I showed you the blood lure?"

He snorted softly. He'd been trying to avoid telling her. But he owed her, and if she knew, it might make her more receptive to his instructions.

"I think he's here, Silver," he said quietly. "The Bush Man."

She stared at him in silence.

"You mean…Kurtz Steiger?" she said, finally.

"Yes."

She reined in her horse, and stopped. "You can't be serious."

He halted beside her but said nothing, letting it sink in.

"You *are* serious." She glanced sharply up at the sky, as if it held some answer. Then she leveled her gaze at him. "What in hell makes you think it's Steiger?"

"The hair you found. The size of his prints. Your description of his physique. The police footwear, the missing sat phones, the feathers left as a calling card, the method of homicide. It's all his MO, the kind of game he likes to play."

"But…his tracks went south, to the U.S. border. That's what they said on the news."

"Silver, what would you of all people do if you wanted everyone to think you went one direction while you headed in another?"

"Leave false tracks. Damn good ones."

"I think he did. And…I think he killed Old Crow."

"What?" She swore viciously. "You think Old Crow died because of this maniac? You think he's come up here for you now?"

"Not just me, Silver." He paused. "I think he might want you, too."

"Why? What does he know about *me?*"

"That you're a tracker. Worthy prey. Female."

She swore again, softer this time. "But why Old Crow…why would he hurt *him?*"

Gabe heard the telltale catch in her voice. Guilt bit at him.

"Maybe Steiger thinks I'm not challenge enough on my own out here. He could have killed someone dear to you in order to invest you fully." Gabe hesitated. "It's the way the Bush Man works. It's consistent with his psych profiles. He's cunning. And very dangerous. And more than anything, he likes to play games…with people's minds."

She stared in stunned silence then swung her horse round abruptly, kicked it forward.

He caught up. "Silver…I'm sorry."

She said nothing. She hid her face from him.

They rode like that for a while, the silence heavy. "What about the rags, then?" she said suddenly, eyes flashing to him. "Why the blood lure if he wasn't trying to hide the evidence from you?"

"I don't know. It has to be part of some puzzle for him. Maybe you can think of a reason he'd do that, something in Old Crow's past, perhaps, something of significance to you?"

Her body tensed. "And now you're going to call in the homicide team?"

"Soon as I get within radio range and can get Donovan to call it in."

"Why can't you investigate a murder yourself? You worked homicide."

Gabe frowned at her resistance to bringing in the dedicated pros. "I'll still be involved, Silver, but it's protocol to bring in a dedicated team of specialists. I've been away from major crimes for a while, and you need guys who are up on the latest technology and clued in to the most current methods of murder trial presentation. That's where you win or lose. At trial."

She shivered slightly.

"Silver?"

"I…I'm just…cold." She kicked her horse faster, galloping well ahead of him as she whistled for her dogs to follow.

A tiny seed of unspecified suspicion unfurled inside Gabe as he urged his mount to catch up and keep pace behind her. She was holding something back. With seventeen years of policing under his belt, he'd become adept at telling a liar. And she was lying.

What worried him was that whatever she was hiding could be key to a lethal game.

One that could cost Silver her life.

* * *

Saddles creaked and bridles chinked softly as they ascended a ridge. The night was otherwise silent, just hooves clicking against stone, horses breathing, and the sound of her dogs panting at their side.

As they crested the ridge, Gabe caught sight of the twinkling lights of Black Arrow Falls cradled in a sea of darkness along a glistening black river. Emotion punched him suddenly in the gut. That tiny cluster of lights was a small symbol of humanity, a home in the heart of the vast, dark wilderness, a tiny tribe that stood together in the face of the elements.

He glanced at Silver. These were her people. And he'd brought danger to their home while he'd been entrusted to protect this place.

He keyed his radio again, anxiety overlaying a growing protective anger. "Black Arrow, do you copy?"

Again, static whooshed, crackled, and then hushed suddenly. Again Gabe got the eerie sensation that someone was listening.

She brought her horse alongside his. "Maybe you're still out of range."

"Yeah, maybe." But he knew he wasn't. "I'll call from a landline as soon as we get down there." He nudged his horse forward, began the descent, an urgency now biting into him.

Silver watched the Mountie heading down toward her village. This couldn't be happening. How could this be the work of the Bush Man? And how on earth could Kurtz Steiger have guessed her darkest secret—the bloodied strips of cloth she'd left blowing in the wind five years ago?

The thought absolutely terrified her.

Because if he *did* know, he was waving it in the face of Sergeant Caruso. And if the RCMP officer called in the homicide detectives, she had no doubt the rags would draw a stark parallel to David's death. The homicide team would look at her again—*she* was the one constant in both deaths now.

She couldn't deal with the scrutiny again. She'd die if they locked her up for the old murder. She couldn't be without her land, her dogs. Her freedom.

"I don't believe it!" she yelled as she headed down the hill after him, to convince herself, perhaps. "It's not Steiger!"

He stopped, swung his mount round to face her.

"Why not?"

"I...I don't see how he could have got up here so quickly. How in hell could he even *know* you were going to be in Black Arrow Falls, Gabe? He only broke out of prison the night before you arrived."

"You don't know him like I do, Silver. This guy is a survivalist. Black ops–trained. His skill is to move fast and efficient, to infiltrate foreign countries in hostile environments. He can be invisible, moving like a ghost in the night. He's also a highly intelligent psychopath, a manipulator of people and information, and he would have been no different in the pen. He could have learned of my posting through the prison grapevine. Knowing Steiger, he would have been watching me from inside."

"Maybe you're just obsessed, Gabe. Have you considered that? Maybe you're seeing him in every goddamn shadow because you can't let go of what he did to you."

He glared at her, eyes glinting in the moonlight, his chest rising and falling.

She'd hit a raw nerve in him, and it buoyed her. It was far easier for Silver to hit back with anger than to allow fear to cripple her. Than to allow herself to hurt.

Or to mourn her son.

Not once since she'd buried his battered little body had she cried. She'd fought back instead—and she'd be damned if she was going to stop now.

She was going to beat this mounting terror in her heart. She wasn't going to allow some ghostly specter to beat her.

And she sure as hell wasn't going to end up in jail because of him!

"You don't think a man like Kurtz Steiger could make it

up here, hide out in these woods for as long as he damn well liked?" Gabe's eyes gleamed in the dark as his voice matched hers in fervor.

Guilt twinged unexpectedly in Silver. He was being forced to confront something ugly, too. A tiny bud of compassion began to unfurl inside her. Dammit. She *was* becoming emotionally tied to him. Was that what this monster wanted, too? For her to fall for the cop who could put her away?

"I know exactly how a man can move through these wilds, Gabe." She said quietly. "I know how people can survive almost forever without coming across another human being in this wilderness. I…just don't think he's here."

"Then, who do you think did this?"

"Maybe…maybe some crazy-ass prospector, some whiskey-addled sourdough who's been hiding in the bush too long. Maybe he came across Old Crow's camp, and—"

"And just happened to be wearing RCMP mukluks?"

"He could have raided a cabin, stolen them down south."

"And left a raven feather in a locked storage shed where three satellite phones used to be?" Gabe cursed. "Silver, the RCMP sat phones are gone, too. They were taken from right inside the detachment in broad daylight."

She shut her mouth, tightened her fists around her reins. She didn't *want* to believe it.

She did not want to accept that her best friend in this world had fallen prey to a cunning psychopath. And now she and Gabe were joined—with Steiger—in some bizarre psychological game that had begun before they'd even known they were being watched. Manipulated.

Hunted.

She felt ill. "Could be coincidence," she snapped, kicking her horse forward and cantering into town ahead of Gabe, suddenly wanting distance from him, and zero part in this "game."

But she felt a cold wind chase her down the mountain

along with the sound of his horse's hooves galloping behind her, a looming sense of evil encroaching as the first winter storm began to roll in from the west.

Chapter 9

Silver stopped at the first dirt road on the periphery of town. Breathing hard, she turned and faced Gabe. The temperature had dropped below freezing, clouds shunting in front of the moon now.

"Take the horse," she said, huddling deeper into her jacket. "I'll pick him up tomorrow."

Gabe hesitated. "I need you to come back to the detachment with me—"

"I need to be alone," she said simply.

"Silver, there's a dangerous man out there. One who might want you—"

"I don't buy it. And even if the Bush Man is out there somewhere, I refuse to play his game. You told me he feeds on fear. Well, he ain't gonna get that from me, Sergeant." She wheeled her horse round.

He grabbed the reins.

She shot him an angry look.

"Silver," he said quietly, firmly, holding her horse. "I can't let you go home alone. Not now. Not until I've asked you some more questions so that I can file a proper report. Not until we get a better handle on what's going down here."

"I can protect myself," she said softly.

His eyes held hers, challenging. And she felt herself wavering.

She glanced away sharply. She *needed* to be alone. To think about Old Crow. To say a Gwitchin prayer for his soul, burn sweetgrass. To grieve in her own way. In private. She couldn't—wouldn't—let Gabe see her pain.

"Silver, listen to me," he said gently. "I've lost people under my care because of this man, because of mistakes I made in relation to him. Don't force that on me again. Don't make it impossible for me to do my job or to keep you safe."

Guilt torqued her heart. She understood what he'd gone through in Williams Lake. She'd never wish that on anyone. Not if she could help it.

"Look, Gabe," she said quietly. "If you are right about this, you're the one who brought the danger here. I think I'm safer away from you."

In more ways than one.

He glanced up at the sky, then he leveled his gaze at her. "I care about you, Silver," he said, very softly. "You've been through a traumatic experience. And for more reasons than one, you shouldn't be alone right now."

Emotion surged sharp and sore. She tried to swallow against the unfamiliar sensation burning in her chest.

This was a good man. A good cop. He'd been through more than his fair share of personal hell, and he wasn't out to get her for her past. He was out to get a psychopath who had harmed countless people, destroyed so many lives. Gabe deserved better from her.

But she also knew she was on a head-on collision course— with her own emotions, with him, with the homicide team he was going to bring in, with an old murder she could still be tried for. And her overriding urge was simply to flee.

Or she could go back to the detachment, entangle herself further with RCMP Sergeant Gabe Caruso, and pay the ultimate price in the end.

Her freedom.

Whichever road she took tonight, she knew there could be no turning back from this point.

She raised her eyes slowly and met his. "Gabe—"

"I need you, Silver. I could use your help." He made it sound somehow intimate, a request no innocent person could justifiably refuse.

But she wasn't innocent.

"I have one officer down," he reminded her. "The others are out of town. I'm the only cop within five thousand square miles right now, and you were the first on the homicide scene. You're the closest thing I have to a CSI out here until we can fly forensics in tomorrow."

Damn him.

He was changing tack, trying to give her an illusion of control, making it her choice to cooperate.

Part of her really did want to help him. She wanted justice for Old Crow—she owed it to her mentor. And an even deeper, more complicated part of her ached to test her reaction to Gabe Caruso's touch again.

But a stronger voice was screaming inside her, warning her that this was a cop who *was* going to find out what she'd done.

How much would he care for her then?

What good would that do Old Crow?

Conflict clawed inside her.

She yanked her reins free from his grip. "You'll manage," she said abruptly. "And I'll be fine. I have my dogs—"

"Please."

She stilled.

Her horse shuffled under her, snorting softly into the frozen night air. Silver swallowed, and against her better judgment, before she could change her mind, she swung her mount round and followed him into the deserted town streets.

Gabe dismounted and looped his reins over the post in front of the detachment building. A stray cat dashed out from under the store across the street. A lone dog barked somewhere in the night and coyotes, prowling hungry on the edge of town answered in a series of bone-chilling yips.

"I'll wait here," Silver said, shrugging deeper into her jacket atop her horse, wishing she'd brought gloves.

"No. I need you to come inside. They might ask for forensic details on the phone—about the tracks, how you found the body. I'll need your help to answer them." He reached his hand up to her, waiting, eyes glinting in the dark.

He was lying. She was sure of it. They weren't going to ask for those details now. But he wasn't taking no for an answer, damn him.

Her heart beat faster as she stared at his hand. It was steady as a rock. Strong. A bridge.

She looked up into his eyes. He was watching her intently, every ounce of attention focused on her. So seductive, in so many ways.

The idea of going into that detachment building freaked Silver out. She felt trapped in there. It brought the terrible memories tumbling back uncontrollably. Gabe was forcing her further and further out of her comfort zone, pushing her places emotionally she hadn't been in years, and she wasn't sure where she'd crack.

Discord churned hot and cold in her belly. The scar on her chest itched, reminding her that she could never fully erase the past, no matter how much she tried. Or wanted to.

Silver hated hiding. She hated carrying the self-imposed label of criminal around her neck. It colored everything she did, and more than anything, she craved absolution. But she'd never get it from a Mountie. He was law enforcement, and in the hands of a Crown prosecutor and the eyes of an unsympathetic jury, she could be convicted of breaking the very laws he was duty-bound to uphold. There was just no way around that.

She hesitated on her horse, momentarily immobilized.

He clasped her hand firmly, making the choice for her, and breath snared in her throat.

She was playing with fire. But damned if she could turn back now.

She swung her leg over her horse and dropped down, landing hard into his arms, against his chest, his scent, his strength, his masculinity, and warmth suddenly and completely enveloping her. Her heart began to gallop wildly, panic and adrenaline thundering through her blood.

He looked down into her eyes, and she could not look away.

For a startling moment his lips came lower, and Silver's madly racing heart stopped abruptly. She braced. He was going to kiss her again. Heat speared to her belly, and she began to quake inside.

But he swallowed, stepping back suddenly.

And something in Silver sank cold and fast.

She inhaled shakily, realizing at that very moment she'd wanted nothing more than to feel the sensation of his lips against her own again, to experience that vivid, crackling sense of hot, vibrant life.

It made her eyes water. It stole all her thoughts. And she just stood there for a moment. Stunned.

"You okay, Silver?"

"Yeah." She breathed out shakily. "Yeah, I am. I...I'm just a bit shook up."

His eyes held her for a moment. "Me, too," he whispered, almost inaudibly, and she wondered if he'd even said it at all.

But his confession endeared him to her. He was both strong

and gentle. Maybe his strength was his kindness, his compassion his power. She'd never met a man quite like Sergeant Gabriel Caruso. Someone who could be alpha and in control, yet not feel a need to subjugate her, to steal her autonomy. He seemed to accept her strengths. She suspected that he understood her weaknesses, too.

And he was making her care about him, making her want to be a part of his team.

That's when Silver knew she was in deep trouble.

It was warm inside the detachment.

Gabe flipped on the lights as he went toward the phone in the reception area. "After I place this call," he said, picking up the handset, "I need you to come with me to check on Donovan. Then I'll take you home."

Silver wasn't listening.

She was standing, staring down the corridor, toward the room where she'd been interrogated for David's murder five years ago, questioned in connection with the death of her own son.

They thought she could have done it—killed Johnny—her own child. The boy she loved with her entire being, loved more than life itself.

They didn't know her. No one did.

You could never really know another person's heart, what breaks her down, or what gives her strength. How she defined courage, rebellion, or success. Not until you'd walked in her moccasins.

That's what her mother had always said.

Coldness crept stealthily into her chest as she continued to stare down the corridor, her world narrowing, darkening to a tunnel between past and present. Before it could suck her back completely, she ripped her mind away, turning to watch Gabe instead.

But her tension only mounted when she caught sight of his face.

"What is it?"

"It's dead," he said, holding the receiver of Rosie's phone. He depressed the bar on the cradle, released. "Stone-cold dead." He pointed to a desk in the office area. "Try that one."

She pushed through the half door, picked it up. No dial tone. She reached for the phone on the next desk. Silence.

She caught his eyes. "Maybe the town satellite dish is down," she said.

"Has this happened before?"

"Once, when there was really bad weather one winter but—"

He was out the door.

She raced after him. It was well below freezing and icy outside now, the first tiny flecks of snow beginning to fall.

Gabe directed his flashlight up to the roof. The RCMP communication antenna, the dish, it all looked the same as it had when he'd arrived.

With his beam of light he traced the heavy PVC piping that covered the wires and cables running down the side of the darkened log building…and swore violently.

Someone had sawed right through the PVC casing and cut the entire bundle of cables, about the thickness of an arm.

"He was here," Gabe whispered. "While we were out on the plateau, he was here cutting the wires."

He spun round, darkness, a madness growing inside him as he probed the frigid night with his flashlight. It had been a ploy, part of Steiger's game, God damn it. He'd lured Gabe into the wilderness while he'd lurked around town to do this. He'd pulled Silver—an innocent civilian into this. He'd killed a man…and he was just getting started.

"Gabe?" Silver rested her hand on his arm. God, she felt good. Real. Steady.

She placed her palm against the side of his face, forcing him to meet her eyes. Her touch was incredible, cool. It stilled his body, calmed something wild rushing through his heart, his mind. Her eyes held his. Crystal clear. And he felt the anxiety subside.

"It's okay, Gabe," she said. "Maybe it's not him. This *could* still be something else."

But he knew the hair DNA would ultimately show this *was* Kurtz Steiger. He knew it with every pound of his heart.

Yet she was reminding him to stay clearheaded, open-minded.

Damn, he'd unraveled for a second, in front of a woman he was supposed to keep safe. But that's exactly what had done it. *That's* what unraveled him—the fact he hadn't been able to keep his own fiancée safe from this madman. And now he was being forced into a replay with another woman. God help him if he lost someone else… God help him if Silver got hurt.

He closed his eyes for a moment.

Silver was his compass in these northern wilds, his anchor. He needed her more than he realized.

"Thank you," he said quietly. "You're right. I was letting it get to me."

Which was exactly what Kurtz Steiger wanted.

He expected her to pull her hand away then, but she didn't. Instead, her eyes softened at his candid words, and in them he could see something deeper. A physical yearning. One he shared.

That mutual awareness simmered softly between them, hinting at something burning much more fiercely underneath. Somehow they'd become allies, bonded over the death of her mentor.

With a killer playing matchmaker.

How absurd, how bloody ironic was that? That Steiger could be driving them together.

Only to destroy them both.

Gabe held that possibility vaguely in the back of his mind as he felt her lean up, lift her face to him. Her lips feathered his and his world dropped out from under his feet, leaving him floating for a moment, an electrical spark crackling through his brain, carrying on a current to his heart, making it beat faster, harder, as his breath grew lighter.

He drew her closer, angling his head and deepening the kiss.

Maybe this was what Steiger wanted. Maybe they were playing right into his hands. But even that black thought was not enough to force Gabe to pull away from Silver. Or her from him.

As their lips met in the cold, pockets of warmth escaped from openings in their jackets, wrapping them in a cocoon against the arctic night, and Gabe thought he might have died and gone to heaven.

To be held again in a woman's arms again filled him with such aching sweetness it burned. It cracked open the lonely prison of the past year, offering him a taste of absolution. Hope. Freedom. It felt so damn human, so *right*. There was nothing—absolutely nothing—in this world that could compare to how he felt at this moment, in spite of the darkness and cold and danger closing in around them.

She wrapped her arms around him, her lips moving silky and warm and soft against his mouth, his mind floating, blinded to all but the sensuality of her skin against his. He wanted to hold on forever.

Nothing else mattered.

He slid his fingers up the side of her neck, into the thick silky hair at the base of her braid, tasting her deeply, her for-eignness, her wildness. He'd forgotten what it was like to kiss a woman. How sweet the world could taste.

She met his need, her tongue teasing the seam of his lips. Gabe moaned, his groin hardening as he drew her more firmly against his body, inhaling the scent of lavender in her hair, feeling the soft swell of her breasts under her coat, the firmness of her lithe body. It consumed him. He forced her mouth open wide, his tongue entering her mouth hungrily, and she stilled suddenly.

Dead still.

As if coming to her senses.

She jerked back sharply, barriers slamming up around her, eyes wide, panicked.

"Silver?" His voice was thick. "Are…you okay?"

"I…I…" She backed away from him quickly, confusion clouding her features.

She seemed at a loss for words. She placed her hand over her mouth. He noticed that she was shaking, her eyes beginning to glimmer with emotion. She spun away, started striding towards her horse.

What in hell just happened here? Had he misread her kiss, her touch? Yet she'd made the first move.

"Silver!" He called going after her.

She untied her horse, unable to look at him.

"Silver, I…I'm sorry," he said, not knowing what else to say, but needing to say something before she shut him out completely.

She set her boot into the stirrup and swung herself up into the saddle. Gathering up her reins, she nudged her horse forward. "You wanted to check on Donovan." She kicked her heels, and she was gone, hooves clattering into the night.

Gabe swore to himself as he ran up the steps, hurriedly locked the detachment door.

What in bloody hell was wrong with him?

He was in uniform. Armed. On the job.

He'd wasted time kissing her instead of going straight to check on Donovan, whose cabin was several miles out.

His constable needed to know that the Bush Man was here, and Gabe needed to know if Donovan's winter RCMP-issue boots were missing. He also had to find a phone that worked.

He swung himself onto his horse, kicked into a gallop after Silver, heavy black clouds darkening the moonlight that had shown their way minutes earlier.

* * *

The wind-ruffled surface of Deer Lake glistened black behind the fingers of skeletal trees.

No lights showed in Donovan's cabin as they approached. His shed door was open, the ATV inside.

The screen door banged against the wall in frigid wind.

Clap, clap, clap—the sound eerily reminiscent of the tent flap slapping against the teepee on the plateau.

They dismounted quickly. Gabe drew his weapon. Flashlight leading, he edged round the side of the cabin through shadows.

He motioned for Silver to stay behind him, registering at the same time she was already tracking alongside the cabin with her own flashlight, her dogs lying obediently with the horses.

"He was here, Gabe," she called out in a whisper. "Same mukluk prints."

Gabe cut his flashlight, motioning for her to do the same. All rules went out the window with a guy like Steiger. Gabe didn't want to be illuminated for target practice until he knew what had happened here.

He stepped onto the porch, and the old wood creaked loudly under his weight. When he tried the cabin door, it was unlocked. Edging it open, he waited, listened. Silence greeted them. Reaching around the wall, he flicked on the lights, swung inside with his weapon leading, his heart hammering.

The cabin was empty.

Cold.

The heat had been turned off, and the windows flung wide open. A breeze toyed with the edge of a red-and-white-checked tablecloth.

There was also bad smell. A sick smell.

Silver entered behind him. Gabe saw she had her twelve-gauge ready, her magnum rifle on her back. She'd left her dogs outside.

"Donovan!" Gabe called, leading into the small passage with his Smith & Wesson, confident Silver had him covered.

After seeing her with that bear, he'd trust her with his life in any combat situation. He'd never come across anyone quite that cool under fire. She was instinctive, the best partner he'd ever had, and she wasn't even a cop. That said something.

"Donovan!" he yelled again, urgency creeping into his voice.

Hollow silence swallowed his sound. The screen door clapped in the wind.

Gabe moved carefully along the wall, and swung with his firearm into the small bedroom.

Nothing moved. The room felt empty.

Gabe flicked the light switch.

His constable was sprawled over the bed, mouth open, still as death.

Chapter 10

Gabe rushed to the bedside. "Donovan!" he said, grabbing his constable's shoulders.

The man stirred, moaned. "Th…thirsty." His speech was slurred. His lips and nails were blue, his breathing light and rapid, his skin sheened with sweat. The scent in the room was horrible, as if he'd been throwing up. And something else, sickly sweet. Gabe felt the man's pulse. It was thready.

"Get some water!" he yelled to Silver.

Silver moved quickly into the kitchen as Gabe reached for the phone at the bedside.

No dial tone.

The line was dead. Just like the RCMP building. Gabe's muscles clenched. He felt Donovan's forehead.

"He's burning up," he yelled to Silver. "Phone's down. We need to get him to the clinic ASAP."

Gabe took the man's face in both his hands and shouted, "Donovan! Can you tell me what happened?"

Silver came running, placed a cold, wet cloth over his forehead.

Donovan's eyes flickered open. "Oh…God….I…I cansh shee.." He sounded drunk.

"Did you take a satellite phone from the detachment, Constable? I need it. I need to call the hospital, get you some help."

The constable registered a moment of lucidity, before his eyes closed again. "Table…phone ish…on table. With…radio."

Silver ran into the living room. "Phone's not here!" she yelled. "Radio's gone, too!"

Gabe's chest tightened.

Steiger had been here.

He'd cut the landline, taken their last satellite phone along with an RCMP radio. He'd been listening in to Gabe's futile attempts at communication. His heart hardened with rage.

"Listen to me Donovan—what happened? Did you see anyone? Talk to anyone?"

He groaned, head lolling to the side.

Gabe quickly removed his personal protection kit from his gun belt, immediately began CPR.

"Gabe—"

He jerked his head up at the ominous tone of Silver's voice, the heels of his hands continuing to depress Donovan's chest.

"I found these next to his fridge." She held up a bottle of antifreeze and a solitary black feather. "He's been poisoned, Gabe. With ethylene glycol. It could have been put in the pineapple juice he's got in the fridge. There's an empty glass in the sink that smells like juice. I've seen these symptoms in dogs who've licked antifreeze. You've got to get him to the clinic immediately. There's nothing more you can do here."

He started to gather his constable in his arms. Silver helped him carry Donovan out.

"I'm going to take his ATV," Gabe said as they staggered over the porch with Donovan's dead weight. "It'll be quicker along the road, easier to balance him in front of me. Follow right behind me with the horses!"

Gabe straddled the seat of the ATV. There was really only room for one, and he struggled to balance his limp constable between his arms in front of him. The snow was coming down thicker now, flakes cold against his skin. He goosed the machine, sending it bounding over the rutted dirt track, bush closing in on either side, headlights haphazardly catching the occasional gleam of an animal's eyes in the dark.

Anxiety clawed into Gabe, and he prayed Silver was close on his heels. Steiger could still be near, waiting to ambush her.

Triage, Caruso, think triage!

His officer was dying, and fast. She had guns. Horses. Dogs. She was a skilled hunter. She handled combat with a cool head. She knew this land. And even if they'd taken the horses and ridden together, Kurtz could still ambush them. It made no difference except this way Gabe might buy the few extra seconds needed to save the life of an RCMP officer under his command.

He swore, thinking of Williams Lake, how Steiger had hamstrung him into making risky decisions.

As soon as he got Donovan into the hospital, if Silver wasn't right on his tail with the horses, he'd go straight back and find her.

The wind was biting hard, driving snow stinging his cheeks as Gabe banged loudly on the clinic doors.

No one was opening up.

Then in dim light he saw the sign on the door—the health care centre closed each night at 8:00 p.m.

Gabe left Donovan bundled up on the quad as he raced round the side of the small hospital building to what he hoped was the doctor's house in back. He slammed the flattened base of his fist against the wood door.

Lights went on. A dog barked.

The door flung open, a man pulling on his sweater over pajamas peered out into the snow.

"Are you the doctor?"

"Yes, Dr. Dave Zeglinski. What is it?"

"I have an officer down," Gabe said. "I think he's ingested antifreeze."

The doc hurriedly pulled a coat on. "Where is he?"

"Out front."

"Phone my nurse," the doctor ordered as they wheeled Donovan into E.R. "Meredith. Her number is on the emergency board next to the phone in the reception area."

Gabe rushed down the corridor to the phones, snagged the receiver…and went cold.

The phones at the health care centre were down, too.

He replaced the handset, a dark dread oozing into his stomach. He picked up another phone, and was greeted by the same hollow silence.

"The phone lines are down," Gabe said, approaching the doctor in ER.

"I need my nurse." Zeglinski didn't look up as he spoke. He was concentrating on injecting Donovan with something. The constable had already been hooked up to machines that monitored his vital signs, and a tube had been inserted into his nose.

"Where can I find her?" Gabe said.

"The house two doors down from mine," the doctor said, removing the syringe.

Gabe hesitated. "Can…you help him?"

Zeglinski met his eyes. "I've given him ethanol, to try and reverse the effects of the ethylene glycol. And I'm doing a gastric lavage through the nasogastric tube. But…" he hesitated, taking in Gabe's uniform, weighing up how much to say.

"Caruso," Gabe said. "My name's Sergeant Gabriel Caruso. I'm the new cop."

Zeglinski nodded. "The prognosis will depend on how long ago he ingested the antifreeze and on how much he took in. Even a few ounces can be deadly. But I must warn you, Sergeant, even if he does pull through the first twenty-four hours, he could still be left with permanent kidney or brain damage, or vision loss. You should contact his next of kin."

Gabe held the doc's eyes.

He didn't want to tell Zeglinski that might not be possible, that the entire town may have been cut off from all communication. But there was no reason to alarm anyone yet. Not until he was sure. There could still be other means of communication available in Black Arrow Falls, other sat phones in the community.

"I'll get your nurse," he said quietly. "You just look after my man."

And he left.

The nurse had been summoned. Donovan remained in critical condition, and there was nothing more Gabe could do. His constable was in the best care possible. His priority now was Silver.

She had not shown up at the hospital.

Fists tense on the handlebars, Gabe barreled back down the dirt track, the tires of his ATV slipping in thickening snow, flakes whirling at him like asteroids in his headlights, wind cutting into his cheeks.

Silver wasn't at Donovan's cabin. Neither were her horses or dogs.

Anxiety roiled in Gabe's stomach as he quickly panned the ground with his flashlight. He could see no sign of any presence at all, fresh snow lay smooth over any trace that may have been left.

He'd never been a position like this—on the job with absolutely no form of communication. No backup. Nothing.

He couldn't do this on his own—take care of a whole town. Not with a psychopathic killer stalking the community.

He needed to check the satellite dish, see if the entire village really had been cut off. Then he'd have to find Chief Peters, tell him about Old Crow's death, see if the band office had any sat phones. He still had hope he'd be able to make contact with Whitehorse before daybreak.

But first he had to find Silver. She remained Gabe's top priority before alerting the town.

With a sick dread growing in his stomach, he punched his quad along the snow-covered trail that led through the forest around Natchako Lake, toward Silver's cabin.

Through the trees he could see that her porch light was on, and his heart raced with a mix of anticipation and anger that she'd disobeyed him.

Dogs barked inside as he approached her porch and clumped quickly up the stairs, flecks of snow numbing his cheeks. Fatigue and the cold were making his old leg injury bother him again.

He banged on the door, her dogs going crazy as he stomped snow from his boots.

No answer.

He cupped his hand and peered through the frosted window. He could see Valkoinen and the other two wolf dogs in there. A fire crackled in the hearth. She had come home, so where in hell was she?

"Silver!" He banged again, dogs going wild inside. There was no way she wouldn't hear those dogs, even if she was in the shower.

Horrible thoughts crept into his mind from a dark place. He glanced behind him. The forest around her cabin was still and dark and dense. A perfect place for a killer to hide. And wait.

The snow was coming down heavily now, big fat flakes swirling and catching light from the porch, rapidly covering any tracks that might have been left.

A perfect time for Steiger to make his move.

Memories of Williams Lake and the snowstorm and deaths there pummeled him.

Then suddenly he caught a glimpse of light through trees as branches heaved in a gust of wind. Outbuildings! Stables. His chest clamped. Of course, she'd have to stable the horses, water, feed them.

He raced down through the drifts toward the warm glow of light in the trees, drawing his sidearm and slowing as he approached the old barn. Just in case.

Gabe crept around the side of the building, snow swallowing his sound, but just as he shouldered open the barn door, it swung back sharply, throwing him off-balance and causing him to lurch forward into the barn.

Silver stepped into view, the barrel of her shotgun pointed dead at his chest.

He froze. "Whoa!" he said, raising his hands slightly.

"Christ, Gabe," she hissed, eyes glinting furiously as she lowered her weapon. "You spooked the hell out of me. I could have shot you!"

"What in hell do you think you're doing running off like that?" he said, holstering his gun, adrenaline slamming though his body. "You were supposed to follow me to the goddamn clinic!"

Her eyes narrowed. "I saw spoor leading from Donovan's cabin," she said, coolly. "I wanted to track whoever did this before snow covered his prints."

"Jesus, Silver. Do you have any idea what this guy is capable of? Do you have some kind of death wish going after him by yourself like that?"

Her mouth flattened. "I wasn't going to hunt him," she snapped as she turned away from him, propping her shotgun against a stall to pick up a bucket of feed. "I just wanted to see which direction he was headed so we could try and pick up his trail tomorrow." She poured the feed into a trough, her jaw tense, her muscles wired.

She was angry. Confused. Afraid. Mostly of her own intense feelings for Gabe. So yes, when he'd gone ahead with Donovan on the ATV, she'd taken the gap and gone her own way. After she'd followed the tracks as far as the creek, she'd come back home. Alone.

It had been a raw impulse. And yes, maybe it had been damn stupid.

"Silver," he said, taking a step toward her, his voice lowering gruffly. "There isn't going to be any *we* picking up his tracks tomorrow. I'm calling in reinforcements. I don't want you trying to mess with this guy."

Her eyes flared to his. "Oh? So *now* you don't need my help?"

"Not to go after him, no. That's police business."

She set the bucket down. "This is the North, Gabe," she said quietly, watching his eyes. "The business of an individual belongs to the whole community. Old Crow's death belongs to Black Arrow Falls. It's a crime against *all* of us." She continued to hold his eyes steadily. "Justice is different here."

"Not in the eyes of the law, Silver. It's still the same country north of 60 as it is down south. Same rules. Same courts. Same judges."

Something inside her hardened. She grabbed a pitchfork, stabbed it into a pile of hay, and threw a forkful into a stall.

"Why aren't your dogs with you?" he said, coming closer. "You could at least have your dogs with you for protection."

"They needed food, warmth," she said, jabbing the fork back into the pile, hefting up another load of hay and tossing it aggressively into the stall.

"You just don't get it, do you, Silver?"

She rammed the pitchfork into the ground, spun round. "No, *you* don't get it, Sergeant. Up here in the North, especially in winter, you take care of what sustains you first—your horses, dogs, guns, shelter—or you perish. You're not going to be any help to anyone dead, are you? And my dogs had been going for days. They needed a decent meal and rest. My horses had to be watered, rubbed down, and fed if we're going to use them to track this guy. And yes—" she held up her palm before he could interject "—you *will* need me to help track him. I'm the best there is out here. Better than whoever the hell it is you think you're getting from White-horse."

"Silver—"

"I owe it to Old Crow."

He stared at her with an animal directness that made her insides suddenly hot. Silence pulsed heavy in the barn, the scent of horses and hay warm.

He took a step toward her, and Silver tensed, her heart beginning to race. She eyed the barn door. He was blocking her escape route. She felt ridiculous for even looking for one.

"How…how is Donovan?" she asked, her voice thick as she tried to shift focus.

"He's critical, only time will tell now." He took another step closer to her, eyes intense, dark, hollow. "Just do me one favor, Silver. Don't high-tail it again without telling me where you're going." His voice lowered further. "I was worried sick."

As he came even closer, her palms turned clammy, and her breathing grew shallow. She pressed her palms against her jeans. "I…I'm sorry, Gabe. I didn't mean to freak you out. I…it's just that I haven't had anyone worry about me in a long time. I…don't know how to do it, I mean—"

"It's okay. I do it well enough for both of us." A hint of a twinkle lit his eyes as he held hers.

A hesitant smile touched her mouth.

"So which way *did* his tracks go?"

"Northwest," she said softly. "He crossed the creek."

"Thank you." He reached up, as if to touch her face with the backs of his fingers, but he hesitated and rammed his hands into his pockets instead.

Gabe looked exhausted, and cold. His features were drawn,

his eyes dark hollows. And she really did feel guilty for putting him through additional anxiety. Compassion squeezed inside her.

"Would you like to come inside, Gabe?" she said. "I've got some leftover stew warming." She allowed her smile to deepen. "Consider it a peace offering."

Something unreadable and unguarded flickered quickly over his features, but he controlled the emotion, and it was gone.

"Silver…I know it's late, but what I really would like is for you to come with me to check the communications dish. I think the whole town may have been cut off, and I'm going to need to find a sat phone."

"You mean you don't want to leave me alone again, unprotected."

He sighed. "You win. So I don't want to leave you alone."

She angled her head slightly. "And if I refuse?"

"Then I beg."

She pursed her lips, and saw the twinkle deepen in his tired eyes. The cop had a sense of humor buried under there somewhere, and she felt herself warming to it. "And when you're done begging, when we're done checking the satellite dish, then will you come in for some caribou stew?"

He grinned, and it warmed her. It made her feel good.

"Yeah," he said. "I'd like that."

The ATV headlights threw into relief a small crowd huddled in coats around the fenced-in satellite dish. Snow swirled thickly about them.

Blanched faces turned as Gabe's vehicle approached. Chief Peters stepped forward from the crowd, his eyes grave.

Gabe could see why. The satellite dish lay on the ground, crumpled and folded onto its side. Acrid smoke hung in the air, and a small electrical fire flickered in wires at the base.

He cut the engine, then felt Silver's gloved hand on his, reassuring him. He squeezed back in thanks.

"Chief," Gabe said, striding up to the crowd. The villagers seemed to brace themselves and gather closer together as he approached. He sensed their hostility. He sensed fear of the unknown. Gabe needed to keep them calm. He needed to keep the entire town calm. Stop mass panic.

"Someone blew up the dish, Sergeant," Chief Peters said. "I've been looking for you."

"I'm here. What happened?"

A woman came to Chief Peters's side. "I heard the explosion," she said. "I live right over there." She pointed to a small square house with vinyl siding. The lights were on inside, throwing yellow squares onto snow.

"And your name is?"

"Suzanne Tizya," she said, pulling the fur ruff of her coat tighter against the wind. "It made a whoosh and a sort of *kerplumf* sound. Soft. I expected an explosion to make much more noise."

"Did you see anyone?"

"No," she said, drawing her vowels out. "What's happening, Sergeant? First the Northern Store, then the band office, now this."

Gabe tensed. He didn't know anything about the store or the band office.

The crowd started muttering in Gwitchin.

He drew Silver to his side. "Go calm them down," he whispered against her ear. "Don't tell them anything about Steiger."

"They need to know—"

"*Not* right now."

Her eyes challenged his.

"Silver—"

She held up her hands. "Okay, okay."

He motioned with his head for Chief Peters to step out of earshot with him. "What happened at the store and band office, Chief?"

"They were both broken into earlier in the night."

"What's missing?"

"From the store, dried food. Propane. Pharmacy stuff, some tools. Flashlight, matches. Looks like the propane tanks were used to make some kind of device that blew up the dish. They're still there." He jerked his chin toward the damaged dish.

"And what's missing from the band office?" said Gabe.

"Our two satellite phones."

Gabe swore to himself.

"And my radio was damaged," said the chief. "It looks like someone put battery acid all over it. It's completely destroyed."

"Chief, we have a serious problem on our hands. But you must keep everyone calm. And I need to talk to the town. Can you call a meeting in the band hall for tomorrow morning, around ten?"

"Why? What is it?"

He glanced over his shoulder. Silver was talking to the villagers in Gwitchin, her voice soft and husky. Calm. He drew the chief farther away. "I believe we have a dangerous criminal, an escaped convict, in the area. And I am deeply sorry to have to tell you that Old Crow is dead. I'm treating it as a homicide."

Chief Peters was silent. "This man in the area, *he* killed Old Crow?"

"We haven't proved anything, but I must treat it as a possibility."

The chief glanced at the crowd.

"I need to know if there any other satellite phones in the community, chief—"

"Old Moose Lodge has—"

"The Old Moose phones are gone. I believe this man took them."

The chief's eyes shot to Gabe, the seriousness of the situation sinking in. "What about the RCMP phones?" he asked.

"Missing. I need to know if there are any other phones."

"This is a poor community, Sergeant. Paying for satellite time is not a luxury many of us can afford. And there's no real need for the phones out here. We do a lot of things in the old way, and with the landlines, the radios, and the two satellite phones at the band office, we get by just fine."

Gabe inhaled deeply, the air cold in his lungs. He rammed his frozen hands into his pocket, stomped his feet. "Okay." He didn't like the way this was going. "When does the next mail plane, or the Air North flight come in?"

"Friday is the first time we expect another plane."

"Today is Sunday. No other flights before that? Nothing at all?"

"No. Things get real quiet this time of year."

"What about the satellite dish? Surely that's under remote surveillance by the phone company. They'll see it's down, send someone up to fix it?"

"Quickest they ever get a tech up here is one week. Maybe longer with this storm closing in," said Chief Peters. "It's the first big one of the winter. Forecast says we'll be socked in for a while."

Gabe swore to himself.

Steiger had done it. He'd completely cut the town off from the rest of the world for the next five days.

Silver came up to him, whispered in his ear. "It was him," she said. "Same prints round the satellite dish."

Gabe nodded. "I need you and the band council to tell everyone to stay calm," he told Chief Peters. "Above all, do not panic. Panic is our worst enemy. And can you call that town meeting for me, for tomorrow? I want to talk to the entire town, make sure everyone's warned."

Black Arrow Falls was under attack. And whatever the Bush Man was going to try, he was going to do it before Friday—before Gabe could get help in. The only option Gabe had now was to lure Steiger away from town, away from these people, and get him alone.

He'd come for Gabe. Well, that's who the Bush Man was going to get. Because Gabe sure as hell wasn't going to let the bastard hurt anyone else.

And this time, there would be only one man left standing.

Chapter 11

Silver kicked snow off her boots and opened the door to her cabin. It was warm inside, embers still glowing faintly in her hearth.

They had swapped Gabe's quad for an RCMP snowmobile, picked up winter gear at the detachment, and gone to check on Donovan. The young constable remained in critical condition, but stable.

Gabe had then brought her home, roaring through snowy woods as she'd straddled him, hugging onto him from behind. Silver liked to be in the driver's seat, but tonight it had felt good just to hold on to someone else.

"Come in," she said, holding her door open for him.

His eyes caught hers, held.

Snow dusted his muskrat hat, and although his Mediterranean complexion was drawn, and his eyes dark and tired, his fatigue had opened something vulnerable in his features that made him even more beautiful. Silver knew he was upset about his constable and thinking about those he'd lost at Williams Lake. She also noticed that his limp had become more pronounced as the night had worn on.

"You look about as tired as I feel," she said with a tentative smile, opening her door wider, her pulse increasing. She'd never invited a *cheechako* into her home, and most certainly never a cop. "I still have that food on the stove. You could use some sleep, too."

She knew he wasn't going to go home. Not now. If she didn't invite him in, he'd sit outside in the snow watching her cabin. "You can have the couch," she said.

He studied her face for a moment. "Thank you," he said, stepping into her home, bending down to allow her dogs to sniff him, his rifle still in hand.

Aumu and Lassi body-wiggled around him, but Valkoinen remained guarded, growling softly from a distance as he assessed the stranger in his home.

"Valkoinen's the boss." Silver said, holding her hand out to take Gabe's jacket. "He's old, too. So he can be a little crusty."

"I know the feeling." Gabe glanced up at her and smiled.

His smile reached right into his brown eyes, and it made her heart do that long, slow tumble through her chest again. Silver stilled for a moment, captivated by the change it wrought in his features.

It was the first time she'd seen him smile, really smile, and it made her feel ridiculously special.

"Careful." She turned away quickly to hang up his jacket, feeling the long angry scar pull across her chest as she raised her hands, reminding her of just how wrong things could go with a man. "He'll take off your hand if he has a mind to."

"I don't doubt it."

Gabe went over to the fireplace, limping slightly, assessing her cabin as he set his rifle down on the coffee table.

Silver locked the door, nerves growing taut as his attention settled on the mantel above the fireplace. He bent closer suddenly. "Who's the kid in these photos?"

A rushing noise began to sound in Silver's ears, coupled with a mad urge to flee.

"My son."

He turned swiftly, stared at her.

She could see him trying to figure things out, rearranging them in his head, his mental image of her rapidly shifting to accommodate this new information.

Avoiding his gaze, she swallowed. "He…died," she said, shocked at how her voice still caught thick and low in her throat. "Some time ago."

She really was on a one-way track now, and gathering speed, because Gabe was going to find out—whether she told him or not—that she had been questioned by police in connection with her seven-year-old son's death.

And the murder of his father.

And if she didn't tell him, he was going to wonder why she'd kept quiet.

A new kind of guilt bit into her tension—as if the pain and the memories weren't enough.

She went to the stove, turned on the heat, and stirred the stew too hard and faster than was necessary, her body strung like wire. She waited for the question she knew would follow.

Instead, she heard him drawing back the fire grate, cracking pieces of kindling, and thumping logs onto the still-glowing embers, stoking life back into the flames. He hadn't said a word.

Her heart began to race wildly. She stared intently at the stew, spoon in hand, immobilized.

He came up behind her, and she braced herself for his touch, her eyes beginning to burn with the threat of tears that never quite came—couldn't come. Lord knew she'd tried to let go, to cry, but something inside just kept fighting to hold it together.

"Smells good," he said softly, his breath warm near her ear. *He wasn't going to press her.*

He could see that she needed space, that she'd talk when she was ready. Her body sagged with gratitude and moisture actually pricked behind her eyes.

Maybe it was because he knew what it was like, to lose the one person your life orbited around. He'd also been dragged over the coals in connection with the death of a loved one. A man like that might just understand her.

She could fall for a man like this.

Except Gabe wasn't just any man; he was a police officer. He was sworn to uphold the law as it was written in black and white. And what she'd done was gray.

Very gray.

She turned slowly, tentatively to face him. He tilted her chin up, looked down into her eyes, and bent forward, his lips meeting hers. And he kissed her so softly, so gently, on the mouth, that Silver thought she had melted from the inside out.

She braced against the stove as he moved closer, pressing his body against hers. She could feel his gun belt hard against her belly, the fabric of his bulletproof vest rough against her arm. She moved her lips against his, more firmly, expecting, wanting him to kiss deeper, this time craving the sensation of him forcibly opening her mouth, inserting his tongue.

But he stopped, looked down tenderly into her eyes. "I'm starving," he whispered.

She was shaking inside, her belly hot. "So…am I," she said, her voice husky. She hadn't even known how hungry. For touch. For affection, kindness. Understanding. And more than anything, absolution.

She wanted to feel truly free inside. From guilt.

Her eyes filled with moisture as she looked up into his, and a tear leaked slowly down her cheek. Her lip began to quiver. This guy was cracking her open, making it all come out. She hadn't thought it possible to cry again. She was terrified of what was going to come next.

He reached up, and brushed the tear aside roughly with the pad of his thumb, saying nothing, and again, Silver was incredibly thankful. She smiled shakily. "Plates are in the cupboard behind you."

He removed his flak jacket, hung it over the back of the chair. Silver watched him, unable to move for a moment, the symbolism of him taking off his protection not lost on her. He was making himself at home. In *her* cabin.

Gabe set colorful pottery bowls and napkins on Silver's heavy wood table, realizing just how much he missed a home. A real home with hearth and the scents of good cooking, the camaraderie of family members.

A sad smile sneaked over his lips as he set spoons next to the bowls.

"What're you thinking?" she asked, her haunting blue eyes lucent, her dark braid gleaming over her shoulder as she brought the steaming pot to the table.

"I was thinking that my mother would be impressed."

Her brow crooked up quizzically. "Why?"

"A woman who not only cooks, but shoots and field-dresses her own game as well? Yeah, my mother would be fully impressed. My little sister however—" his smile deepened and his heart felt a little lighter as he thought of the Caruso clan "—is a vegetarian."

"She wouldn't last long up here," Silver said with a smile as she set the pot down. "Hunting is our way of survival, always has been."

"I know." He thought of Steiger and what a different meaning *hunting* held for him. For Steiger it was sport, a thrill, the pursuit of a life with intent to possess it, wholly, for his own pleasure. It was about power. It was about owning another human being fully.

He glanced at the door. He'd seen her lock it, and the

shutters were drawn tight against the night. Her hounds lay near the fire, seemingly at ease, but their ears twitched with each small sound.

Those dogs would be the first alarm should anyone come anywhere near her cabin. His RCMP rifle was on the table, her shotgun and magnum on the rack. His sidearm within easy reach. He felt fairly secure. Mostly because his gut told him Steiger wouldn't attack them here.

It wouldn't be fun.

It wouldn't be a *hunt*.

Gabe would stay for the night and watch over Silver. In the morning he'd take her with him to the town meeting where he'd get some men to agree to play bodyguard, then he'd lure Steiger into the woods.

Alone.

"Is she a good cook, your mother?" Silver asked, seating herself on the bench opposite him, handing him a serving spoon, motioning for him to help himself.

"In the best Italian tradition," he said, taking the spoon and dishing up a bowl full of stew, the rich scent making his mouth water. "Our family revolved entirely around the kitchen. Whatever went right—or wrong—mother's solution was to feed everybody."

"You speak in the past tense."

He stilled with the spoon, feeling guilt.

She angled her head as she studied him. "You have a big family?"

"Three brothers and a kid sister. Nieces, nephews, uncles, aunts, grandparents—the works."

A wry smile crossed her mouth as she took the spoon from him. "It's funny, but a guy like you, a sergeant in uniform come to run the show, you don't automatically think of him having a mother." She began serving herself. "Do you see your family often, Gabe?"

"Not often enough."

Not once since the funeral—neither his family, nor Gia's. God knows they'd all tried to contact him. But he couldn't handle the latent accusation he felt with Gia's relatives, nor the sympathy in the eyes of his own family members as they tried to downplay their own achievements and good news of births and marriages in order not to hurt him or exacerbate the pain of his loss.

They all knew how badly he and Gia wanted children, how they planned to carry on the Caruso tradition.

He'd cut his friends off, too. Apart from Tom and a few other members on the force, Gabe had pretty much kept to himself.

Now he was going to change that. Something had shifted in him. He wanted to find his way back.

But he'd have to finish off Steiger once and for all to get there.

She sat close, but not too close, staring into the crackling flames, and Gabe found a sense of warm, easy comfort doing battle with arousal inside him. He realized with mild shock that he wanted her. Completely. Blood began to pulse in his groin.

He slid his eyes over to her, studying her profile. Silver had showered, and her hair hung damp and loose about her shoulders. She was wearing a soft flannel shirt, fresh jeans, and moccasins, and once again Gabe was struck by her stark, natural beauty, the aristocratic angles of her cheekbones, the copper brown of her smooth skin.

He swallowed, unsure of himself. Or her. She was a paradox, and she confused the hell out of him. He recalled the confident slash of a smile she'd flashed at him back at the airstrip the day he'd arrived, compared to the hesitant curve of her lips when she'd welcomed him into her home a few hours ago. He thought about how she'd kissed him confidently, then run scared the instant he'd taken a dominant role.

Gabe sensed a fiercely guarded privacy and very real vulnerability behind Silver's independence.

It made him wonder what she hid underneath. It made him want to know her better. *Much* better. And the extent of his need surprised him.

When it came to women, Gabe had to confess to a streak of dated thinking. He believed in soulmates, and he'd believed he'd found his in Gia. When she died, it blew a hole right through him. He never dreamed there would be someone beyond her, that he might feel these stirrings in his blood and heart again. It both exhilarated him and made him uncomfortable.

He tore his attention away from her profile and glanced up at the photos on the mantel again—Silver and her son—and wondered about the child's father.

But Gabe knew how tired he got of incessant questions about his own loss, how they scooped him hollow. He hated the helpless look in people's eyes when he told them what had happened. He detested the impotence that came with the impossibility of assuaging their discomfort at seeing his grief. It was far easier not to talk at all.

So he didn't voice what he really wanted—to ask Silver about her son, her past loves. He respected her privacy. Still, it didn't help that he wanted to know everything about her. Intimately so.

"We can track him, Gabe." Her sharp blue eyes flashed to his suddenly. While staring into those flames, she'd been thinking of Steiger. "We can hunt him down, flush him out."

"And then?" he asked, mildly bemused.

But her eyes glittered cold, dangerous, like her wolf dogs, and his heart skipped a beat at the clear and sudden ferocity he saw there.

"There's no glory in killing a man, Silver. Never is, never should be."

She stared at him with a raw animal intensity that made his spine tingle. "You're saying *you* wouldn't shoot him? If you got that animal into a vulnerable position, alone out there in the wilds, with no one to see what happened, no witness to ever know what went down?"

He held her eyes, saying nothing. Aware of his badge, of legalities. Aware of his oath to preserve life. Aware that his weapons had been issued to preserve life, not take it, to be drawn only when confronted by immediate and lethal force.

But Gabe was also aware, fully, that he *would* shoot Steiger, even if it wasn't clearly self-defense.

He wondered when, exactly, he had crossed that line in his mind. And a whisper of dark coolness edged into him.

"That would be against the law," he said quietly, sidestepping the question.

She looked away so sharply, it was as if she'd taken a hit on the jaw.

He reached out and touched her, and she tensed further.

"Silver," he said softly, sensing that she was testing him on some level, disturbed by what might be lurking beneath her questions, uncomfortable at being forced to talk about this in black and white, to be made to look into himself like this. "Don't you see? This is exactly what Steiger wants. For you— for me—to react this way. He's stripping us down to a primal streak, to the survivalist, the animal, in us all. Which is why I can't let you be a part of this. I can't let him make *you* want to cross lines like this. I cannot let you hunt him." He paused. "Apart from safety considerations, apart from legalities and police protocol—it's not going to happen."

She had a strange look in her eyes. "What do you think he's going to do next?"

Hurt me through you. Make me helpless again by forcing me to watch him take a woman from under my care.

He blew air out slowly. "He came for *me,* Silver. I need to lure him away from town, away from you. And I need to do it alone."

"No. You need me, Gabe. You can't do this on your own."

Oh, he needed her all right—he was shocked by how much.

"What I really need—" he said, his voice lowering to a whisper as he leant forward, "—is for you to be here when I get back, Silver."

She held his eyes, her own darkening to a sensual indigo. "You're not going to come back, Sergeant," she said softly. "Not unless I go with you, and help you hunt him."

Attraction simmered, inevitable, inexorable, electric, between them.

She leaned forward slightly, and he hesitated, then closed the distance, firmly cupping the back of her neck, his lips touching hers.

Heat shafted clear through to his groin, and his blood began to thrum in his ears.

She moved her mouth against his, both tentative and hungry, her hand sliding slowly up the length of his arm, her breathing turning light and fast.

Lust peaked hot and sharp and fast, and it stirred Gabe's anxiety that he might move too fast, do something to scare her away again. She was such a complex mix of contrasts. But her hand moved to his chest, fingers splaying firmly against him, and he felt a groan rise from somewhere low in his belly as she slid her hand lower, fingers slipping between the buttons of his shirt, meeting his skin.

He was conscious of his gun within reach, the sound of ice ticking against the window behind the shutters, hyperaware of everything while blinded by sheer bliss at the same time.

He opened her mouth cautiously with his, testing her with his tongue, drawing her down into his arms, knowing deep down there could be no turning back for him now.

Her tongue slicked, tangled, with his as he rapidly unbuttoned her shirt. She had no bra on. His pulse hammered faster. He opened her shirt and smoothed the soft flannel back over her shoulders, exposing her breasts, moaning with pleasure at the warm, smooth sensation of her copper skin under his hands.

He sat back slightly, wanting to savor the look of her naked torso in the firelight. But what he saw made Gabe freeze.

He was gripped by a moment of irrepressible horror at the viciousness of a scar that sliced violently from her left shoulder, puckering across the smooth swell of her left breast to almost her breastbone, mangling the flesh just above her dusky nipple.

His eyes shot to hers.

She began to tremble, her eyes wide. Naked with emotion.

"Who did this to you?"

Her eyes flickered up to the mantel. She drew her shirt closed. "I…it was an accident," she said, almost inaudibly.

"Silver—"

She swallowed, her fist balling the fabric of her shirt tight against her chest. "It's horrible. Ugly. I…I'm sorry." Tears spilled in a sheen down her face catching the light of the fire.

"No, oh, God, no, Silver. That's not what I meant—" he reached to touch her, but she pulled away. "Tell me what happened, what kind of accident?"

She glanced away. "It's nothing."

"Silver?"

"I said it's nothing." She refused to meet his eyes.

She was lying. But why would she need to lie to him about this? What was she hiding?

Yet she had let him see it. As if she'd needed to. Why? To test him?

"Silver, this is not nothing." The wound hadn't been stitched up neatly either, which told him she hadn't gotten proper medical attention when it occurred.

"When did this happen? Who treated you?"

Something shuttered sharply and with finality in her eyes. She got to her feet, the front of her shirt still balled tight against her chest, knuckles white.

"You can take the couch—"

"Wait!" He grabbed her hand, now convinced that someone had inflicted this wound on her.

Her dogs stiffened instantly, heads up, ears cocked, watching Gabe. Valkoinen growled. She quietly ordered them to stay.

"Tell me who hurt you, Silver," he said firmly.

She seemed frozen, unable to answer him. She stared at his hand restraining her wrist.

"Silver, please, listen to me. You are the most beautiful woman I've ever come across. This…" He looked up into her eyes. "This is not ugly. It's the viciousness of it that is. That's what shocks me. It makes me angry that someone could do this to you."

Her pulse raced at her smooth neck.

"I need to know who did this to you, Silver."

Panic, fear, or whatever it was that haunted her, tightened her features, made her eyes bright. "I told you," she said softly, "it was an accident."

"It was a man, wasn't it? And he hurt you deeper than that scar, didn't he?"

She began to shake. "Please, Gabe, let me go."

He released her wrist.

She spun round and made for her bedroom door. It closed with a soft snick.

Gabe forced out a chest full of pent-up air—rage, regret, compassion, desire, simmering in a dangerously volatile cocktail inside him.

Every instinct in his cop's body told him that whoever had sliced her chest open had also hurt her in the most intimate way possible.

Judging from her reaction to his questions, to physical intimacy, she'd very possibly been raped.

A raw, fierce will to protect this woman boiled up inside Gabe, all his anger narrowing onto one target—Steiger.

He could *never* let him near Silver.

If he got her, he would hurt her in the most terrible ways possible, making her relive whatever it was that still haunted her now.

Gabe reached for his rifle; cradling it, he leaned his head back against the couch, listening to the storm outside. He fingered the trigger softly. He'd kill anyone who tried to touch her.

He was going after Steiger, and he was going to finish the bastard off. It was wrong. But Gabe was beyond that now. He was in a new place, where old rules wouldn't apply.

And when he came back, he'd find out from the villagers what had happened to Silver. He'd check Black Arrow Falls' old police files for a record of the assault, and then he'd go after whoever did this to her.

He wasn't going to push her to tell him herself. Whatever had happened, she'd clearly suffered enough.

And it explained so much about her.

It explained why she'd pulled back from his kiss the moment he'd taken the driver's seat.

If he was going to love Silver, he was going to have to cede her all the control.

And that's when he knew that Steiger had already won this round.

Because he'd just given Gabe something to lose.

Again.

Outside in the darkness, the wind whipped flakes that stung into his skin as he hunkered down under the swaying branches, watching the cabin. He welcomed the discomfort. Just as he embraced the now-continual throbbing pain in his leg where his wound was growing red and swollen.

Pain is my friend. Patience the art of the predator.

Light seeped faintly through cracks in the wooden shutters. Smoke curled from the chimney. It was late, and they were in there together. Maybe by the fire.

A smile curled along his mouth. Yes, the Mountie was fully vested, but he wasn't so sure about the tracker. Yet. Perhaps she needed another incentive.

Something that would snap her, break her control completely. Bring out the animal within—the animal he wanted to challenge himself.

And he'd been watching her long enough to know just how to make it happen.

He felt for his hunting blade…

Chapter 12

Silver braced her hands on the bathroom sink, glaring at her tear-stained face in the mirror.

She was such a goddamn idiot.

She wanted him. She wanted so desperately to feel his warm body against hers, to feel him inside her.

Heat pooled in her belly, and the tears came again. She began to shake. She clutched the edges of the basin, gritting her jaw, trying to pull herself together.

Gabe had released her. He'd cracked her out of some emotional prison, enabling her to feel again. To cry. To want. To yearn. It was such an incredible catharsis, but instead of allowing him to touch her, instead of going all the way, she'd run.

You bloody coward!

She ripped her shirt back off her shoulders, let it drop to the floor, and stared at her naked torso, the savage scar over her breast, her hair hanging down over her shoulders.

The shock—the horror—in his eyes had been the worst.

It had made her feel so unattractive, undesirable. So ridiculously broken.

She tentatively touched the puckered ridge of skin with her fingertips. It *was* ugly. Violent.

Like her life.

She traced the rough edges, following the hideous trough David had gouged through her flesh with a jagged piece of rusted tin.

He'd thrust her backwards, rendering her almost unconscious as her head hit a rock. He'd assaulted her, violently, sexually, while the small, bloated body of her boy lay dead and unseeing within an arm's reach.

Her stomach retched. Tears began to roll faster and a racking sob escaped her chest, a noise she didn't even recognize as coming from within her, from somewhere buried so deep, like a petrified fossil coming to life, surfacing, ripping her open from the inside out.

Her heart began to thump.

Perspiration beaded on her brow, and she gripped the basin tighter, closing her eyes for a moment, but that was worse.

It just made the memories more vivid.

David had passed out, drunk, thinking he'd already killed her. He'd come to as she was trying to crawl away. His gun was just out of his reach, but she'd seen him moving for it. Her survival instincts kicked in and she'd acted first.

She'd killed him before he could kill her.

An unsympathetic jury might not see it that way. A defense lawyer might not be able to convince them that David would have killed her if she hadn't moved first.

Silver was convinced David had been a psychopath. Initially he'd charmed her, blinded her, but he'd been using her. He'd been a bootlegger who needed a base in town, and she was it. His liquor trade had ultimately brought pain and destruction to the people Silver loved. And those villagers who suspected what she'd done to David didn't speak about it. In their minds, justice had been served. David had paid the price for his sins.

She'd put the blood lure into branches to attract wildlife, hoping to destroy the body. It had worked. There was not enough evidence to charge her, even though the RCMP suspected she could have done it.

But the guilt was still there. Like her scar, it would never go away.

And Old Crow's killer somehow knew. He was making it fresh, making her relive the horror. Forcing her to take a cop along for the ride.

Her jaw tightened, and her eyes hardened. She glowered at her reflection. She'd made a terrible mistake with Gabe.

As an RCMP officer, Gabe Caruso was one of the few people in this country who had been granted the authority to take from her the one thing she cherished most—her freedom.

While he may have set something emotionally free inside Silver, he still had the power to physically imprison her.

If she confessed to him, he'd be faced with only two choices. Handing her over. Or becoming an accomplice after the fact—a criminal himself.

She could never put him in that position.

Silver wasn't sure when exactly it had happened—maybe even from that first moment she'd looked into those rich brown eyes and seen an echo of her own lonely pain—but she'd come to care deeply about Gabriel Caruso. Confessing to him would force him to confront who he was—either an RCMP officer, or her lover. Because he couldn't be both. There was just no way either of them could come out of that one unscathed.

A banging sounded abruptly on the bathroom door. "Silver!"

She froze.

He banged again, louder. "Are you okay?" She heard the hard bite of worry in his words.

She couldn't find her voice.

"Silver!"

Her heart began to pound. She didn't know what to do. She hurriedly wiped her face, not sure if she could face him right now.

"Silver!" He heaved against the door and it cracked open against the wall.

She gasped, hands bracing behind her on the sink as he thrust himself into the bathroom, rifle at his side. Shock registered on his face as he saw her naked from the waist up.

"Dammit, Silver! Why didn't you answer me! You were quiet for so long, I…thought…" His eyes swept over her breasts, her bare stomach, and he dragged his hand over his hair, not knowing where to look. "Are you okay? Why didn't you answer?

She still couldn't seem to find her voice.

His eyes fixed on her breasts, on her scar.

She swallowed, refusing to hide, to cover herself up again.

Raw desire darkened his gaze as he stared at her. She shivered slightly, her stomach tingling. He didn't find her repulsive. He still wanted her. Intensely. It was etched into his features, in the way his hand trembled slightly as he set the rifle down on the bathroom counter.

"Silver," he said, voice thick, rough, as he stepped closer. He reached up and gently touched her scar with his fingertips. "Don't ever think this makes you unattractive." He traced the ridge slowly down toward her nipple. "Don't ever do that to yourself," he whispered, fingering her nipple between his thumb and forefinger until it peaked so tight it hurt. "You have nothing to hide, not from me."

You don't know the half of what I have to hide.

She held his eyes, her breathing growing fast and shallow. Then she moved forward suddenly, her lips meeting his. She kissed him hard, opening his mouth under hers, her tongue seeking, slicking with his, as she moved her hand up the side of his torso, feeling the ripple of muscle under her fingers.

He groaned, cupping the side of her head, fingers digging into her hair but allowing her to take the lead.

It fed her confidence. Her hunger.

She wanted him. She wanted to try and be with a man again—with *this* man. She reached for his shirt buttons, fumbling to undo his uniform, desire consuming her, burning away any anxiety about the future, blinding her to everything but this moment. She didn't want to think anymore. If she allowed herself to think, she'd let the fear back in.

He moved his hand down the length of her waist, his rough palm trailing a wake of tingling nerves over her bare skin. Heat speared between her thighs. She felt herself sag back against the counter as her limbs turned limp. He kissed the base of her neck, his tongue tracing the hollow under her throat. She threw her head back, trusting him. He kissed the skin on her chest, his lips soft and warm and wet against her breast as he took her nipple into his mouth, circling it with his tongue. Silver began to shake.

She splayed her hands against his pecs, feeling the coarseness of his hair under her palms, the solidity of his muscle moving under supple skin. She ran her palm down his abs, fingers exploring the hard ridges, the whorl of thick, dark hair that ran into his pants, meeting the hard leather of his gun belt.

He pulled back suddenly, and her heart nearly bottomed out.

"Come," he said, his voice thick as he encircled her wrist. "Come back to the fire."

Gabe set his gun belt on the coffee table with a soft clunk and unzipped his pants. Silver watched him unabashedly from the rug in front of the fire. And she could see that her brazen scrutiny made him even harder. She liked what she was doing to his body—it fed her strength.

Silver had never had a problem with fear and insecurity before David.

David, though charming at first, had damaged her. He'd made her feel ugly. A pariah.

Gabe was giving her back something of herself, and her heart ached with affection because of it. She knew what he was doing right now—stripping himself completely in front of her. Leaving nothing hidden.

Leaving every little move up to her.

She knew in her heart that he would stop if she felt insecure, or frightened. And he wasn't going to press her about her scar. Or her son. He wasn't going to corner her.

Silver had never come across a man like Gabe. And she was sunk. Fully. Totally.

She also knew it couldn't last.

But she didn't want to think about that right now. What he was giving her was too precious. He was making her whole again.

And he was utterly beautiful in his nakedness. Powerful. Thighs and chest strong. Firelight shimmered over his olive-toned skin, outlining his muscles, throwing into shadow the thick, sensuous, dark whorl of hair that arrowed to his groin.

He knelt before her, his erection solid, and she noticed that he had scars of his own, along the inside of his calf and thigh. Steiger had done that.

She looked up into his eyes, a bond growing in her heart.

The wind howled outside, rattling at the shutters, as blowing flecks of ice tapped against the frosted windows.

Her dogs slept silently, as if they knew she was safe.

Gabe reached up and moved her hair back from her bare shoulders, appreciation glimmering in his features, and he smiled at her.

Her eyes misted again. He made her feel beautiful. He made her feel like a desirable woman again.

She reached up, drew him down to her, and he angled his mouth against hers as she undid her zipper, slid her jeans and panties down over her hips.

Tongue slicking gently with his, she opened her legs to him, and she felt his breath catch in his chest.

"Are you sure, Silver?" he murmured against her lips.

"Very," she whispered, raising her hips, an aching heat throbbing low in her belly.

He ran the flat of his hand down her stomach, slowly, very slowly, inching toward the inside of her thighs. "Tell me," he whispered, "if you want to stop."

She answered by covering his hand with her own, guiding it lower as she began to shake with need, with the quivering anticipation of being touched again for the first time in five years.

His fingers moved between her legs, and cupped her gently, warm. She inhaled sharply.

He stilled.

But she opened her legs wider, lifting her hips higher to him, easing access, delirious with the need to feel more of his touch. Slowly he began to caress her, parting her folds open a little more each time, movement growing more slick, firmer, as she grew hotter. Then he slid one finger up inside her. Slowly.

A cry escaped her throat.

He stilled.

She shook her head. "No," she whispered. "More, please. I...want you, Gabe."

He slipped his finger deeper, began to stroke a part of her that made her want to cry out again. She dug her hands into his back, opening wide, arching her back.

He trailed his lips down her stomach, and holding her thighs open with his hands, he kissed her between the legs, flicking with his tongue, entering her.

Tears ran down her face. She couldn't contain the release. She was shaking so hard.

She arched desperately up to him. She wanted him, all of him.

He positioned himself between her thighs, lowering his weight gently over her, and she felt the hot, smooth tip of his erection.

For a moment, fear tightened, but he eased into her, filling her, and her mind swirled.

He gradually pushed deeper, allowing her body to accommodate, and then he began to move, the pace achingly exquisite, driving her higher and higher.

Silver forgot everything. She forgot her fear, the fact he was a cop. She allowed the moment to consume her as she tilted her hips to him, opening wider, moving under his body, matching his motion with her own, feeling the roughness of his hair between her legs.

He took her cue, thrusting faster, harder, each time to the hilt, driving her wild. Sweat slicked over her body as it slid under his, his chest hair deliciously rough against her bare breasts, his weight bearing down on her heavily.

She froze suddenly as her muscles gripped tight, then she shattered under him with a sharp cry, tears streaming down her face.

He let himself go, shuddering into her, holding her body so tight she felt nothing in this world could harm her.

She laughed and cried, emotion overwhelming her, everything she'd held back for five long, bad years releasing in his arms.

He stroked her hair back from her face, kissed her. And the look of tenderness in his eyes broke her heart. Everything that defined this man—why he'd become a cop, his fierce compassion—it was all there in that one unguarded moment of expression, and in that instant Silver loved him.

This man would protect her with his life—and she was going to have to break his heart.

Because she couldn't ask him to change who he was.

She couldn't ask him to choose between her and being a cop.

Chapter 13

Dawn arrived gray and cold. It would be some hours before the northern sun poked above the horizon.

Gabe stood at the window, dressed in his uniform and flak jacket, nursing a mug of coffee as he watched Silver's dogs cavorting outside like kids in the fresh powder. A smile sneaked into his heart, and the concept of family and future lodged into his brain.

He wanted to try and make a go of it with Silver, and for that he needed to get through the next five days—alive. He adjusted his gun belt. He was ready.

He'd talk to the town at the meeting. Then he'd gather his gear and leave Black Arrow Falls.

"Gabe?"

Silver stood in her bedroom doorway, freshly showered and incredibly, radiantly beautiful.

His heart torqued.

Making love to her had been like coming home. Silver had

given him what he'd lost—desire for a future. She'd made him want to reconnect with his family.

She'd made him think of all those things that had felt so ridiculous after Williams Lake. Of all the things he'd ever wanted.

"I'm not letting you go alone," she said, her cobalt eyes piercing him from across the room. "You do know that."

He said nothing.

There was no way in hell she was coming with him.

There was just no way he was ever letting Steiger near her. Ethically, he couldn't let *any* civilian come with him. If he had his choice he'd lock her up with a phalanx of armed guards outside the door.

He'd talk to Chief Peters, ask him who would best guard Silver, knowing at the same time making her stay was going to be a challenge.

Her features tightened. She walked into the kitchen, poured coffee, set the pot down hard suddenly, glared at him. "He knows more than you out there, Gabe. He'll trap you, kill you."

He sipped his coffee, watching her.

"Damn it!" Her eyes glittered. "You're not planning on coming back, are you?"

His heart thudded soft and steady. He didn't want to reveal any emotion now. He had to be the cop he was trained to be. "I just need to lure him away, Silver," he said calmly. "Just long enough for one of the planes to get in Friday, and the chief can get word out to Whitehorse. If I can keep Steiger busy until then, we'll have the military in, infrared heat-sensing choppers, the works. I'll be fine."

She glowered at him. "I know what you're doing. You're sacrificing yourself, aren't you? For this town, for me." Her eyes shimmered with emotion. "It's not bloody fair! You can't do this!"

He set his coffee down. A few days ago he'd have been fully ready to sacrifice himself, but not now. Now he wanted to win so goddamn bad he was almost blinded by it. Steiger had no idea what he'd done by pushing him and Silver together. He had no idea what ferocity he'd created in Gabe by giving him something to lose again.

Maybe, just maybe, this time Steiger had actually orchestrated his own demise.

He came up to her, took her shoulders, holding her steady as he looked down into her eyes. "I have *every* reason to want to come back, Silver."

Tears spilled silently down her cheeks.

"Damn you, Gabe Caruso," she said softly. "Look at what you're doing to me!" She spun round, reaching for her jacket, punching her arms into the sleeves. "If you really cared about me, you'd take me. You'd allow me to do what I do best. You'd respect me as a partner. You wouldn't try and make me sit at home like…like…some pathetic worried spouse!"

He blinked.

She rammed her hat onto her head and her feet into her boots. "You better go somewhere else to get horses, because I'm sure as hell not letting you take mine on your suicide mission." She grabbed her guns from the rack beside the door.

"Silver, you need to come with me to the meeting."

"You want to go after Steiger by yourself? Handle the damn meeting by yourself."

He reached for her.

"Don't." She held up her palm. "Do not touch me. You don't own me. You don't control me. You can't make me do anything. And don't think I won't shoot you if you try."

She slammed the door behind her, whistled for her dogs.

Gabe grabbed his gear, went after her. "Silver!"

She stomped through the snow toward the stables, ignoring him.

Conflict ripped through Gabe. He couldn't leave her on her own, yet he also knew she was right—he wasn't going to force her to do what he wanted.

He had to get some men to watch her. Fast. And he had to get the hell out of town and lure Steiger away even faster.

Gabe swore viciously as he plowed his way through the fresh drifts toward his snowmobile and fired the engine. Blue smoke coughed into the icy air, and he opened the throttle wide, barreling along the lakeshore and into town.

"You need to protect yourselves," Gabe told the crowd. "Consider this guy armed and dangerous, and do not approach him under any circumstances. He is special ops–trained and skilled at unconventional warfare, meaning guerrilla tactics. You need to move in groups, and I want you to keep all children inside, at all times."

Gabe paused. "Above all, try not to panic. He's come for *me*. I will lead him away from this town, and no one here will be in danger."

"Then why must we arm ourselves?" Someone yelled from the back. "What are you not telling us, Sergeant?"

"It's a precaution. Just to be safe until one of those planes comes in, which will be in five days unless we get lucky and someone flies in sooner."

Silver leaned against the doorjamb at the back of the packed hall, arms folded, watching.

"As soon as a plane comes in, Chief Peters here will get the pilot to send word to the Whitehorse RCMP detachment, and there will be police and military choppers in Black Arrow Falls within two to three hours. You will be safe then. All of you."

Murmurs started among the crowd, growing louder. Someone yelled in Gwitchin, pointing at Gabe. "He did this. He brought this evil to Black Arrow Falls. He's a curse." The mutterings grew louder in agreement.

"Yes," said a big youth near the back. "First Old Crow dies, then the constable is poisoned. Who is next?"

"Why should we trust him?" a woman called out.

Chief Peters held up his hands, trying to quell his people.

But the crowd grew noisier, agitated. A baby started to wail. Silver could see Rosie sitting in the corner, tears in her eyes, fear on her face, her two young children clutching her skirt.

Silver knew her people. She knew how close to the surface the spiritual and magical lived. This Bush Man was assuming superhuman qualities in their minds, and their fear was being fed by mass hysteria, along with an innate distrust of outsiders. Like the RCMP.

Like Gabe.

And they were turning on him.

She pushed off the doorjamb, strode calmly down the centre aisle of the hall, back held straight, her braid hanging square down the centre of her back.

The crowd hushed as she stepped onto the small stage beside Gabe and Chief Peters. It was so quiet you could hear a feather drop.

Silver was as much an enigma to the Black Arrow Nation as she was to outsiders. Yet she'd been accepted. Her mother had been a well-loved member of this community. Her father had embraced them fully.

So had she.

This was her home, and she considered these people her family. They had protected her after David's attack. David's bootlegging had brought evil and corruption to town. They'd considered what happened to David justice, Northern style. She had no idea how many elders suspected her true secret or knew the extent of her injuries, what she had suffered at David's hand. But some did. Chief Peters did. They knew that Silver, out of all of them, had the most reason to distrust the RCMP, because they'd failed to help her by not searching for her son when she'd asked for their help. And she had the most reason to fear the police, because they'd then turned around and tried to prosecute her for David's death.

They also knew that in her heart, Old Crow was the most dear.

So when she stood by Gabe, the message was clear. She trusted him.

"You must do what he says," she said in Gwitchin, her voice clear and strong. "Sergeant Caruso didn't bring this man to Black Arrow Falls by choice. Let him catch this man. Do not let Old Crow's death be in vain. Help the sergeant do his job. Help him look after this town." She caught Gabe's eyes, switched to English. "He has our interests at heart."

And mine.

Edith Josie in the front row nodded. Jake Onefeather stood up, and he also nodded. Rosie got to her feet holding her children's hands, one in each of her own. The employees from Old Moose Lodge slowly rose to their feet.

"She's right," Chief Peters said loudly, stepping forward. "It has been our elected band council's choice to contract with the RCMP, and we must stand by our decision. We must trust the sergeant. We can do this. For hundreds of years we, the small Black Arrow Nation of the Gwitchin, have protected ourselves, and we will do so again until help comes in five days. We must listen to what Sergeant Caruso has to say. And we must do what he advises."

"Thank you," Gabe whispered into Silver's ear as the chief spoke, and her eyes burned.

But she didn't look at him. She said nothing. She stepped down off the stage and left.

"We have lost telecommunications," said Gabe, taking centre stage again as Silver walked down the aisle, feeling his eyes boring into her back. "But we still have electricity, gas, and diesel supplies. You must now form groups to guard these essential services—the diesel-generating plant, the health care centre, the airstrip. You must protect food and water sources. Keep your children indoors and your animals safe. Protect your transport—"

Silver left the hall, the double doors swinging closed behind her, cutting the sound of his voice.

Her heart thudded softly. Her chest was tight. She wasn't going to sit around in that hall waiting for him to go on a suicide mission. She whistled for her dogs.

Only two came.

She called again for Valkoinen. But only the soft rush of wind through the frozen streets greeted her. She whistled and called again. Silence.

Panic hooked into her heart.

Where was he? He'd come into town with her—he would never have left of his own accord. Something had to have happened.

Silver whirled round, scanning the ground for her animals' tracks. And what she saw shot ice through her veins.

She swung her gun off her back, clicked off the safety, and ran down the street through the drifts, eyes fixed on the fresh spoor in the snow.

The trail led her back to the lake, through the woods—to her own cabin.

Exhausted from her trek through the snow, panting hard, lungs burning, sweat dampening her body, she pushed open the door of her barn.

And in a heartbeat, everything changed.

Gabe lugged his gear onto his porch. It had been snowing again since the meeting, and another few inches of the white stuff covered the ground. His snowmobile was filled with gas, and he had reserve fuel and supplies in a small cargo sled attached to the back of his machine. He'd packed carefully, and he wanted to be gone well before noon. This light wasn't going to last, and there was another snowstorm in the forecast.

He locked his door, but stilled at the sound of horses approaching.

He clicked the safety on his rifle, and walked to the end of the porch, vaguely concerned that the rabble rousers from the meeting might have gotten a mob together.

He froze when he saw it was Silver.

She had three horses. She was riding one, the other was saddled, and the third packed with gear and feed. She was dressed for heavy weather with the flaps of a fur-lined hunting cap pulled down over her ears.

He lowered his rifle slowly, watching her face. Something was wrong.

She looked haunted, hollowed out, and filled with something sinister. His pulse kicked.

"Silver?"

She said nothing as she drew her horse up alongside him. Gabe tried to read her, his eyes flicking quickly over her gear. She had two magnum rifles, her shotgun, tent, shovel, tarp…no dogs. He hadn't seen her once without Valkoinen right at her heels. His chest tightened, and his eyes flashed up to hers.

"Where are your dogs? Where's Valkoinen?"

Her lips thinned, and her eyes glittered fierce in the monochromatic winter light as she glared down at him.

Oh, God, no.

"Silver, talk to me. What happened? Did he hurt your dogs?"

Her jaw jutted out, as if she was trying to hold something in by sheer defiance. "I'm going after the Bush Man," she said, her voice strange, cold. Dangerous.

Gabe spun round, dragging his hat off, swearing violently as he kicked the porch post.

He should have left last night. He began to shake with rage inside, then whirled back to face her. "I can't let you do this. I *won't* allow you to hunt him!"

"I'm not asking for your permission, Sergeant. Are you coming or not?"

"Silver, I'll be forced to take you in if you try and do this. Don't make me do that."

She glared at him, waiting.

Then she swung her horse round sharply, and clucked her tongue as she kicked her mount forward.

"Silver, *wait!*"

Hidden high on a basalt cliff, he watched through the powerful scopes he'd taken from the small Beaver before sinking it into the frigid depths of Wolverine Lake, the pilot strapped naked in the seat. The pilot's fur-lined Yukon cap now kept him warm, as did the man's jacket, gloves and other gear.

Steiger was confident no one would be looking for the missing man yet.

He caught sight of the small posse crossing the snow-covered valley several miles out. Three horses. One carried supplies. The Mountie and the tracker were mounted on the others.

No dogs.

Steiger smiled. He'd slit the throat of only one. Her favorite one. She was obviously taking no chances with the others.

He tucked the scopes into his pouch.

The tracker was fully vested.

The hunt was on.

Chapter 14

They trekked northwest, toward the black massifs along the Alaska border.

Stunted conifers speared along distant granite steppes, but a little farther north, in the Barren Lands, the ground was treeless. A pale sun trapped in a nimbus of ice crystals hung low on the horizon. Several feet of snow blanketed the ground, but the biting wind had ceased and the air hung deadly still, all life suspended in frozen anticipation of the next storm.

Their horses' hooves crunched through the crisp crust that had formed on the powder. Silver had sold Gabe on the merits of traveling on horseback rather than snowmobile. Although slower, it was easier to track from a horse, she said, and snowmobiles would ultimately run out of fuel. Even if they ran out of grain for the horses, at this time of year, the animals could still forage beneath the snow. They could be gone for weeks.

His chest was tight as he rode behind her. She'd taken the

lead, scanning for spoor, her braid hanging thick down the back of her fur jacket, puffs of mist from her breath condensing in the frozen air. Gabe covered her from behind, rifle cradled in his arm as he scanned the rolling white plains and black ridges with his scopes for small signs of movement.

Although snow had blanketed any tracks the Bush Man may have left, they were heading in the direction Gabe had seen the small plane go down.

Silver's eyes had turned positively glacial when he'd told her the location of the plane's descent. "Wolverine Gorge," she'd said. "Near the abandoned mine." The information seemed to have set her course. She said the mukluk prints leading from Donovan's cabin had pointed in exactly the same direction—northwest.

Gabe was concerned about a trap. The only spoor Steiger ever left was the kind he intended you to find, but Steiger didn't know that Gabe had seen the small plane struggling, so he couldn't have factored that into his plans. Their primary goal was now to detect fresh signs of the Bush Man— anything at all that might give them an idea of what he was up to. And even if they didn't find a trace, Gabe knew they were leaving a blazing trail of their own.

Steiger would find them.

He wished to God Silver wasn't with him.

But she was out of his control. Valkoinen's death had made her reckless, and she was hell-bent on going after Steiger with or without him.

Gabe exhaled heavily, his breath frosting. He wondered if he should have stuck her in lockup, under guard, for her own safety.

Vigilante justice was against the law, north of 60 or not. And by not taking her in, he was allowing her to endanger herself both physically and morally. He also knew he'd do exactly the same thing in her shoes.

He was in a double bind, sinking deeper and deeper into gray policing territory with each step forward. Because if he were truly honest with himself, Gabe knew he had a better chance of finding—and taking—Steiger with Silver's skills.

He swore softly. That was probably exactly what Steiger had anticipated. By taking the life of Valkoinen, he'd sucked her over to a dark place, investing Silver fully in his game. Gabe feared she might never be the same.

At least this way he stood some chance of protecting her. From the Bush Man. And from herself.

Gabe peered up at the distant ridges with his scopes, squinting against the angle of the pale sun. He had his police radio with him, but Steiger had one, too—the one he'd taken from Donovan's cabin.

It linked them.

Gabe could communicate with the psychopath if he chose to. He half expected Steiger to make contact with them at some point, find a new way of taunting them. Gabe had ordered Rosie to maintain complete radio silence, even though they'd be going out of dispatch range. He didn't want to alert Steiger to the fact that help was imminent, when—if—it came.

All they had to do was stay alive for five more days, until that help arrived.

Gabe clenched his jaw, nudged his heels into his horse, catching up to Silver. "We've been going for five hours and seen no trace of him at all. Why are you so certain he went in this direction?"

Her eyes caught his, ice-blue diamonds under the gray fur ruff of her cap. His heart ached. She'd refused to speak further about what happened to Valkoinen since they'd left Black Arrow Falls, and Gabe was at a loss as to how to open her up. All she'd said was that he was dead. Aumu and Lassi had been spared.

Steiger had seen enough to know that Valkoinen was her special one. And by sparing the others, he'd let her know it, making the attack more intimate, personal.

"We're going this way because it's where you saw the plane go down, and it was the direction his tracks led from Donovan's cabin," she said.

He shook his head. "Don't mess with me now, Silver. We're both beyond that. And I'm not a fool. Something more is setting you on this route—what is it?"

Her eyes hardened. She rode in silence for a few moments. "There's an abandoned gold mine up there," she said. "My father took me once. He used to work there some summers before I was born. Several men died working that mine, and the locals say it's haunted, so no one ever goes anywhere near the shafts anymore. The mine has a geological fault that makes it dangerous even now, and a fugitive could hide in those tunnels for months, years even, without anyone finding him."

"That still doesn't explain why you think Steiger is there."

She shrugged dismissively, rode on, a little faster. Gabe came alongside her again. "Silver?"

She blew out a hard breath of air, and her eyes flashed sharply to his. "It's where my son died,"

"Whoa." He reached for her reins, halted her horse. "What happened to your son, Silver?"

The wind stirred suddenly, carrying fresh snowflakes on a puff of frosty breath as the sky closed in on them. Hooves squeaked in dry snow as the animals moved restlessly under them, sensing the abrupt shift in weather, the coming storm.

She shook her head. "I…can't talk about it, Gabe. You of all people should understand. I…just think this is part of Steiger's game. Maybe he wants me to relive something, okay?"

Tension snapped across his chest. "No, it's not okay. What in hell makes you say *that?* Did he leave you some clue that this was the case?"

She said nothing.

"Silver, I didn't want to press you, but now you have to tell me. If you think your past is somehow woven into Steiger's game, I need to know what that past is."

"I—it's nothing. I…I'm probably just imagining stuff."

A hot spark of exasperation flickered inside him. This woman had been hurt. She'd been horribly scarred. She was a mother who had lost her son. And now she was being pushed well beyond her limits. Gabe felt he had no right to push any more out of her. But if her past was directly tied to the present—to their future—he *had* to know what happened.

"You're hamstringing me, Silver," he said coolly. "I can't fight this battle if I don't know what I'm fighting. We can't be a team if you're going to hide things."

"Maybe," she whispered, "it's my battle to fight."

"No, Silver. This is our battle. This is about *us.*"

He caught the telltale glimmer of emotion in her eyes as she cast them down. She hesitated, fiddling with the reins. "My son's name was Johnny," she said quietly. "He was seven years old. He drowned, up at Wolverine Gorge, near the mine."

Gabe felt as though a rock were being pressed onto his chest. He couldn't breathe. He didn't know what to say. "I…God, I'm sorry. How…how did it happen?"

She inhaled slowly, looked up, into the gathering flakes of snow, the wind starting to blow. "His father took him without my consent. We were estranged. His name was David. He flew back into Black Arrow Falls that summer to sell booze, and he was on something, some drug. He was a well-known bootlegger up in the North, Gabe. He was also an alcoholic. He took Johnny while I was out guiding. He picked him up outside of school on the last day before the summer holidays, leaving a message for his caregiver saying they'd gone on a short camping trip and that he'd okayed it with me." She looked away. "The caregiver called me on the sat phone right away, and I rushed back. I was home the very next day, Gabe. But my boy was gone. And David wasn't stable. I went straight to the RCMP, and told them Johnny had been abducted." Her eyes narrowed. "They sat on their asses mumbling about custody and paternal access and a bunch of bloody crap while my son was in the woods with a drunk who was high. So I went after them myself. Tracked them up there—" She tilted her chin toward the ominous northwest ridges. "To Wolverine Gorge."

"What happened?"

"I didn't track fast enough. There'd been an early summer rainstorm, a flash flood. The gorge is known for this. David should have seen the signs. The bastard had taken Johnny fishing in the water there, God alone knows why. He was spaced out of his mind, didn't see the water rising, and…"

She cast her eyes down again, voice choking.

"Silver—" He reached to touch her hand.

Her eyes flared to his. "I don't want sympathy, Gabe. I just think Steiger is there, that's all. Where Johnny died."

She wasn't thinking straight. She was having some kind of post-traumatic reaction.

"Silver, Steiger couldn't know—"

"The story was in all the Yukon papers. It'll be in the archives. He could have found it."

"It doesn't make sense, Silver. Not unless he left something to clue you in to a connection, to let you know this was the game he's playing. That's his MO."

She glared at him, bottling something in with forced anger, and his stomach sank.

"He did, didn't he? He left you a sign? Where? When? Why the hell didn't you tell me?" He swore. "This changes everything."

Little did he know just how much.

Every molecule in Silver's body burned to tell him the whole truth.

If they made it through the next five days, Gabe was going to find out anyway. And anything she'd shared with him up until this moment would be over.

He'd despise her for hiding the truth. For lying by

omission. For hamstringing him, as he called it. It wasn't fair to him.

It was also potentially dangerous.

She *had* to tell him. But she just couldn't make herself do it right this minute.

Silver was terrified of going to prison, yet more than anything, she didn't want to see the disappointment in Gabe's eyes. She so desperately wanted to be something she wasn't—for him—but she wasn't going to be able to hold onto that dream anymore.

It was over. She had to face that.

Without warning, the storm seemed to explode around them, the opaque sky suddenly thickening with snowflakes that whirled and shimmied like dervishes on gusts of frozen wind.

"No," she lied, blinking back snow melting against her skin. "I didn't see any clue. I'm making an educated guess that he's up there, that's all. It's where you saw the plane go down. The mukluk tracks pointed in that direction, and Wolverine Mine is a good place to lie low. If the Bush Man likes to screw with minds, and if he's seen any archived stories about me…" she hesitated. "Then he might also see some sick symmetry in drawing us up there, to freak me out or something." That was as close as she could go.

But he didn't believe her. She could see it in his eyes.

"I'm sure we'll see some sign of him before long," she said, jerking on the reins and swinging her horse round into the teeth of the storm. "There's an old trapper's cabin up on the ridge ahead," she called, the mounting wind snatching her words. "We can hole up there for the night, until the weather passes."

It would be safe, thought Silver, at least for some hours, because they'd be able to see literally for miles over rolling white snow-covered tussock and muskeg plains.

The storm would also provide cover into the woods. Any tracks she and Gabe were leaving would be gone within minutes.

* * *

Huddled close by necessity, one blanket wrapped over them both, they ate ready-to-eat rations, and drank hot sweet black tea in front of a small fire in the ramshackle hut. Given the whiteout conditions, there was no worry about telltale smoke swirling from the old flue. The horses, accustomed to winter in the Yukon, clustered together under an eave on the leeward side of the hut where they'd been fed.

What had been a void of eerily crystalline silence was now filled with the freight-train-like roar of the storm through frozen treetops, trunks swaying and creaking and moaning against the furious onslaught. Small branches, cones, lumps of ice thwacked onto the old metal roof and lashed against the old wooden walls. Gabe reasoned that they were fairly safe here tonight, yet he felt under attack, like a small wooden boat being hurled about the sea in a frozen gale.

Something cold had settled deep inside him. Where earlier he'd felt an unarticulated bond between himself and Silver, he now felt a distance yawning open between them.

She touched him, her eyes crackling with something dark and mysterious. The desire was there, still hot. She moved her hand down his stomach under the blanket, lower, to his pants, and he felt himself swell. He welcomed the physical connection. As if the heat of passion could ward the darkness off, the secrets. Keep the icy evil at bay.

She needed him in an elemental way, but while it made his blood pump and his stomach tingle, the cold in his bones lingered. He had a sinking sensation that this would be their last time. Not because he wanted it to be, but because of some fundamental shift in her demeanor.

She was hiding something, and it filled him with a sense of ending.

She straddled him, naked from the waist down.

Whatever confidence Silver had lost with sex when she'd gotten that scar was returning, especially if she could take a dominant role, and it excited him, made him exquisitely, painfully hard.

She slid down onto his erection like a hot, wet glove.

It was fast and primal. She moved on him in a way that turned Gabe's mind delirious, aggressively rhythmic strokes up and down his shaft until he thought he would scream for mercy.

But he let her take total control. She was strong, her muscles taut, her inner thighs holding him fast, friction driving him to an excruciatingly sweet pitch as the wind wailed outside. She was hungry, something desperate rising in her, her breaths coming light and fast. He slid his hands down her waist, grabbing hold of her hips as she rode him, pulling her deeper onto him, her long braid over her shoulder, her jacket still on.

She threw her head back sharply as she released with a gasp, nails digging into his shirt. He climaxed at the same time, and she collapsed limp into his arms, her head nestled into the crook between his neck and shoulder.

Gabe reached for the blanket and pulled it up over her shoulders as he held her, still straddled on his lap as he softened inside her. She fit him so well, felt so right. But it was sex, he thought—it wasn't making love. It was hot and fast and fabulous, and he wanted to do it over and over again. But something was missing, as if the part of her he'd connected with had retreated into her shell. Even as he climaxed inside her, he'd felt a sense of loss.

He held her tight, desperate to grasp something slipping away under his fingers second by second the more they traveled toward Steiger, to whatever horror awaited.

She slid off him, the friction arousing him again instantly. Gabe was mildly bemused. He'd thought himself physically incapable since Gia died, but he was finding himself very much alive, he thought as he zipped up his pants.

"Do you want to talk?" he said softly. "About Valkoinen?"

"No." She tugged the blanket over her shoulders and cuddled next to him, her head on his shoulder, facing their tiny wood fire.

He inhaled deeply, putting his arm around her. "You know, Silver, I've been a cop for seventeen years now. You see things, do things that haunt you, sometimes even make you hate yourself. It's not good to hold it in. It eats you like cancer from the inside." He paused. "You need to talk."

She turned to look up at him, watching him intently.

"I know what you're thinking—that I have no right to tell you what to do when I've been bottling up a crapload of stuff myself this past year. But it's *because* of this that I know what it can do to you. When I was with Gia, we talked. Not necessarily about the specifics of a case or an incident, but in general. You need that. You need to let it out."

"You must miss her."

Her comment sideswiped him. He lost his words.

"What was she like, Gabe?" she said softly.

He gave a wry smile, stroked Silver's hair. "She was my soul mate, Silver. I've always held this old-fashioned notion that there was one person out there for everybody, and I believed I had found mine in Gia. I never thought I would—*could*—want anyone else in that way again." He held her eyes. "I was wrong."

She glanced away, pulse thrumming in her neck.

He wondered what was going on in her mind, a frustration growing in him that she was retreating further minute by minute.

She was quiet for a while, staring at the flames as the wind howled outside and loose boards slapped. "Valkoinen had a good life," she said finally, as if trying to convince herself. "He was old, Gabe." She paused. "Like Old Crow…but…" Her lip began to wobble, and she bit it hard, eyes gleaming brightly. Then she suddenly spun to him, tears streaming down her cheeks. "Please…please, could you just hold me?"

"Oh, Silver—" He gathered her against his body, held her tight as the storm pummeled them, and the cabin creaked and moaned and she sobbed, her slender shoulders heaving, her face buried into his chest, tears wetting his shirt. He stroked her hair and held her until she'd sobbed herself dry.

She sniffed, wiping her eyes with her sleeve, hands trembling slightly. Her face was bloodless. "I…I'm so sorry. I…" She looked up at him with red-rimmed eyes, and Gabe's heart nearly broke.

"I couldn't cry after Johnny died. I didn't cry, not once…until I met you." She tried to smile. "You made me cry, damn you."

It was the most revealing thing she could have said to him. It touched him in such a profound way it made his own eyes burn.

When he'd first seen her with Old Crow's body, Gabe had gotten the sense that Silver didn't grieve. She bottled it up and lashed out instead. He hadn't realized she'd been lashing out for five years and was now worn thin, utterly drained.

"Is it because of Johnny that you track kids, Silver?" he said, moving a damp strand of hair back from her cheek.

Her eyes flared to his. "Who told you I track children?"

"Donovan."

"He say anything else about me?"

"Not really. Why?"

"No reason." She hesitated. "And yes, Johnny is the reason I track lost children. I wasn't quick enough, good enough to get to my son before I lost him. I never wanted to be in that position again, Gabe. I didn't want another mother to go through what I had. I needed to be better, faster. I took what skill Old Crow had taught me, and I learned more. I went to conferences, courses, met with experts about missing children specifically. Kids tend to think and react differently from adults when they're lost in the wild. They behave differently when rescuers approach, too. Sometimes they hide, even. So I practiced, I volunteered, and I combined the old ways with the new science. Now I'm one of the best. And I'm quicker."

But still too late to save her son. She was saving other people's kids instead, and in doing so, trying to find resolution, some meaning in her own loss.

He thought of her compassion for that grizzly sow who'd lost her cub, and Gabe understood. And he realized that he loved this woman.

He loved everything about her.

He was beginning to love this land, too—its harsh beauty, its elemental values. The place where he thought he might have come to die was becoming a place he might just want to stay to live. For a long, long time.

"Where is David now?" he asked.

She got up suddenly, went outside, creaking the small wood door shut behind her.

A chill of foreboding crawled over his skin.

He followed her out. The snow had stopped, and the world was muffled silent. The horses snuffled under the shelter, nosing their grain.

She had pulled up her fur-lined hood over her cap, and was holding binoculars in thick gloves, looking out over the snowy plains now bathed in glimpses of platinum moonlight as clouds scudded south.

It was a hauntingly beautiful, eerie, and desolate vista.

He felt her tense as he came up behind her, his boots squeaking in the fresh powder.

"We can't do this without trust, Silver." He paused. "If we don't have trust, we have nothing."

She lowered the scopes, turned, looked him directly in the eyes. "I know," she said softly. "I know."

Chapter 15

It was morning of the second day, and they'd been trekking since before dawn, nearing Wolverine Gorge. Through scopes, the dark shapes of the abandoned mining structures could be seen huddled on the side of the wind-sheared mountain. Silver was following a slight depression in the pillows of snow that covered a wide valley. It was a trail Gabe didn't really see, and it seemed to be frustrating him. Silver believed the barely visible dent was snowed-over spoor.

She stilled her horse abruptly—she could make out some irregularities to her right. She dismounted for a closer look as Gabe forged ahead.

As she scanned the area at the base of some trees, Silver's pulse quickened at what she saw there. She moved, quickly, deeper into the trees, and tensed, her heart beating faster. She shot a look at Gabe. He'd moved several yards ahead. Panic strafed her.

"Gabe! Stop!"

The ice wind tossed her words into the bleakness. He didn't hear, didn't stop.

She reached behind her back, grabbed her shotgun, flung it to her front and fired into the air. It kicked back hard.

The gunshot echoed into the mountains.

Gabe froze.

"Do not move an inch!" She yelled, running and stumbling and falling through the drifts towards him.

"What the—"

She crouched down in front of his horse, breathing hard as she softly flicked snow from the trail with her gloved hand. She stilled, glanced up at him, breathing hard. "He was here!"

"I don't see anything," he said, dismounting and bending forward.

She brushed more snow away, carefully exposing a carpet of cut branches knitted together under the fresh snow. She grabbed the base of one, tugged it back sharply. The others collapsed inward, tumbling into a pit with a soft implosion of powder that sent tiny crystals floating into the sunlight.

Aspen trunks sharpened to lethal creamy-white points speared up from the base of the deep, black pit.

If she hadn't fired her gun, if he hadn't stopped right then, Gabe and his horse would be impaled and bleeding in the bottom of that dark hole this very minute.

"Deadfall," she said. "A trap."

One that could have become his grave.

Gabe swallowed. Reaching for his rifle, he and Silver moved in a slow circle, panning the terrain, squinting in the harsh reflected light.

"There's no sign of him," she whispered. "I can't see any tracks from this point. Nothing at all."

"He must have done this before the storm," Gabe said, lifting his scopes to his eyes, scanning the shimmering white sea of snow. "Steiger knew the snow would cover any sign of his trap." He lowered his scopes. "How in hell did you know it was there?"

"Drag marks on the leeward side of those trees back there. Snowdrifts blew in a funnel around them, leaving the trace exposed. And further into the grove, if you look carefully, you can see trees have been cut, the fresh saw marks rubbed with dirt and covered with snow. He took what he needed from there and dragged it over here."

"Maybe it's just someone trying to trap an animal."

"Wishful thinking. Traps like this are all about location. You position them where you know animals routinely travel, and this is not a game route. This one was for us." She swore. "He's given me a degree of credit, Gabe. He anticipated I'd see and follow that slight depression I've been tracking all morning. He led us right here, set this deadfall bang in our path." She cursed again, viciously, feeling exposed. For the first time, she truly felt like prey.

"I didn't expect him to be so goddamn subtle," she snapped. "I don't like it. I do not like feeling hunted!"

Gabe was watching her intently, his intelligent brown eyes assessing. "He could have heard the gunshot. We should get out of the open, find cover, lie low for a while."

"Not on your life." She pointed at the trap. "This is the first real trace we have on him, I'm not going to drop things now."

She left the trail they'd been following and stomped off towards a stand of conifers, determined to find some sign of which way the bastard had gone after he'd set the deadfall.

"Silver!"

"I said not ye—"

Gabe lurched forward, hitting her square in the back, flattening her into the snow with his full force. Her breath slammed out of her with a whoosh, and her gun discharged as she hit the ground, her finger forced hard against the trigger. The horses reared, whinnied, and bolted.

Silver tried to lift up her head, but Gabe bashed her down fast just as a dead weight dropped loose from high in the branches of a tree and swiped through the air right over their heads, splattering gouts of blood over snow as it went.

Silver's heart jackhammered as the thing spiraled back and spun on its rope, spraying more red over white, the scent of blood strong, coppery. She could smell guts, too.

Her stomach clenched as she stared up from the snow in horror, trying to make sense of the spinning thing, her throat going tight as she recognized what it was—a skinned coyote, studded with sharp metal spikes like a giant flail. It had been strung up in the tree so that when the weight of its body was released by a trip wire, it would fall, the animal's torso dropping lower than the head, forcing the gash at the neck to open wide and gush blood.

Bile rose to her throat. If Gabe hadn't shoved her into the snow, it would have slammed into her, spiked her like some macabre medieval weapon.

Gabe eased his hold on her and helped her back to her feet.

"How…how did you know?" She couldn't seem to speak around the tightness in her throat. Her limbs felt like jelly.

"The trip wire, it was just under the snow over there." He pointed. "It caught sunlight as your boot depressed the powder just in front of it."

She should have seen it, and suddenly she was scared.

The man *was* a ghost.

"It's how he left two hunters," Gabe said, his voice thick and his face bloodless as he stared at the slowly swaying and spinning carcass. "Near Grande Cache, north of Jasper. It was his last kill before…before Williams Lake. He stripped the couple naked and set them on the run. That's how they were eventually found. Strung up in a tree like that, set as a booby trap for the cops."

Silver felt faint.

"He's taunting us, Silver. He's got to be somewhere nearby. Very near."

Silver swore violently, adrenaline mixing with fear and

making her shake inside. "Cut it down," she snapped. "We've got to cut it down!"

"Silver, he could be watching. We should—"

"*No.* There are no fresh tracks around here. He hasn't been back here since the storm. The snowdrift covered the wire, that's why I didn't see it. He's still some way out, and I want this thing down, now. It's a waste. A bloody waste of a life." She unsheathed her own knife when Gabe didn't move.

"This bastard is not a hunter." She reached for the rope. "Hunters don't kill like this. He's a torturer." She cut the restraint and the carcass thudded softly into the snow. She gritted her jaw. "He's worth *nothing!*" She glared at Gabe. "You know what Old Crow would say? He'd say that the land will not tolerate this. The land will get him. He won't last in this place."

Gabe said nothing. He was watching her intently.

"What? You think I'm losing it?" She snapped, worried that she actually was. Worried about her own mounting fear now. Recalling what Gabe had said about the Bush Man stripping his quarry's mind down to the raw basics.

"Go get the horses, Gabe."

"Silver, are you—"

"Just get the damn horses!" She spun round quickly, wiping the back of her glove hard over her mouth, trying to stop the shaking. She didn't want Gabe to see her like this.

She waited until he was gone, and then she crouched down, and covered the coyote gently with snow. She thought of Valkoinen, and tears burned sharp behind her eyes, her jaw sore from trying to hold it all in. What this bastard had done went against everything she believed—to take life like this. She *had* to believe he couldn't get away with this.

She closed her eyes for a second and did something she hadn't done since her mother died. She prayed, silently reciting a Gwitchin entreaty to the spirits. She prayed for Old Crow. For her dog. For her son. And she felt just a little stronger when she stood up, a little less alone.

She walked out to meet Gabe who was returning with the horses.

"We circle out and then we backtrack over our own trail," she said, taking the reins from him and swinging up into the saddle. "I don't think he went farther north along this path. He's not on the run. He's hunting. I figure he set this trap and then retreated. My bet is he'll be on the spoor that we left since morning, coming up behind us right now, to see if we fell for it. If we head out through that valley over there—" she pointed "—and circle round for several miles, we could double back and come up behind him while he's tracking our spoor."

"He might anticipate that," Gabe said, still watching her carefully.

Silver felt sick. It was true. Steiger might give her the credit for thinking up this scheme, too, and be ready.

She finally understood what Gabe meant when he'd said that the Bush Man thought she'd be worthy prey. For Steiger this was like chess. He liked to second-guess, and he relished a good match.

She wasn't sure she had the stomach for it.

They found Steiger's tracks as night began to creep over the great dome of northern sky. A comet sheared off in the distance and tiny stars emerged, twinkling.

It was beautiful, but Gabe felt somber inside as he looked down at Steiger's prints—a clear sign the Bush Man was following them, hunting them.

From the prints, it was evident he was now somewhere between them and the deadfall trap.

The sinister mood affected Silver, too.

They were walking the horses now, tense, slowly crunching through snow that had melted slightly during the day and was setting up hard again as the temperature plummeted.

Silver dropped to her haunches suddenly, studying a particularly clear set of footprints with her flashlight.

"What is the animal thinking, Silver?" she whispered as she bent closer. "That's what Old Crow used to say to me when I was little," she told Gabe, moving slowly forward to the next set of prints, shining her beam of light into the depressions. Gabe followed quietly, trusting her skill. He kept watch over the moonlit terrain while she had her head down. They were working as a team, yet she was still holding something back, and it bothered him.

On more levels than one.

"You must become the animal, Silver," she whispered softly. *"Then you will know how to find him without looking. You will know where he was going. And why he was going there."*

An icy chill shuddered down Gabe's spine. For a strange moment he almost imagined he heard Old Crow's voice whispering from the universe.

"What can you tell?" he asked, more to break the surreal spell than to get an answer.

She stopped, looked up. "I've never had to do this, Gabe, get into the mind of a sick man. I don't like it. I feel like I'm letting him into my soul." Her voice was strange, and Gabe felt himself harden inside.

"Don't think about his mind, Silver, just follow his tracks."

"That's exactly why no one ever catches him," she said. "They don't *become* him. They don't try to think like him when they're reading his spoor."

He didn't know what to say, so he reached down and touched the side of her face instead. "Hey, we can do this," he whispered. "As a team."

She held his eyes for a moment then turned away quickly. "He's left-handed," she said, aiming her flashlight back onto the tracks.

"He is, but how can you see that?"

"From the way he's walking on the right side of our tracks. Usually it would be the other way round. He's looking over his left shoulder as he follows us."

Another shudder of cold chased through Gabe. He could almost visualize Steiger, tromping along, eyes trained on their prints. He didn't like the way everything felt like it was doubling back on itself. A circle they were locked into.

They moved slowly ahead for a few yards, and Silver tensed again, crouching down suddenly. Gabe's pulse quickened. "What is it?"

"He's tiring," she said, fingering the Bush Man's tracks gently with her hand, probing some nuance that escaped Gabe.

She got up, quickly moving off the trail toward some trees. She panned her flashlight over the snow around the trunks and came back again.

"He rested up there, under the branches. I don't think he anticipated us backtracking him, Gabe; otherwise he'd have tried to cover his sign."

"Unless he wants us to see this."

"I don't think so. Something's wrong with him, Gabe." She walked a few feet farther, eyes on the ground.

"What are you seeing?"

"He's been favoring his left leg from a ways back, but now he's actually dragging it, and the drag is becoming rapidly more pronounced. See there? See that mark between each step? It's getting worse. And from the depression depths and the change in his gait, he's showing signs of fatigue."

"He was shot and lost a lot of blood when he escaped max security," said Gabe. "We don't know where he was hit, though."

"Somewhere that's giving him trouble with that left leg. But I didn't see this in his prints back at the plateau. I think his injury has been getting worse since then." She moved off the trail again, back up toward the tree line, her flashlight playing over the snow.

Gabe stayed with the horses, keeping an eye peeled for movement, his gun primed to shoot.

There was a hint of new energy in her step as she returned.

"I think his wound is infected, Gabe, look—" She held out a small wad of matted dark material as she came toward him. "These are pine needles, chopped and steeped in boiling water, and then dumped in the snow. He made a fire back there, and pine tea, lots of it, probably boiling it down as a disinfectant. It also works as a natural antibiotic. This stuff has more vitamin C than a bag of oranges." She looked up at him. "He's sick, Gabe. It could give us an edge."

His pulse accelerated. "Or it could make him desperate."

Silver and Gabe traveled for another hour, tension winding tighter as the night wore on and they got closer to the Bush Man—Gabe edgy, expecting another trap.

He was about to say they needed to stop, and hunker down for the night, regroup, when Silver saw something and stiffened suddenly.

"What is it?" he said, coming up to her.

She pointed. "Bear prints, coming from the direction of that ridge up there. Not just any prints, Gabe." She caught his eyes, her own glittering feverishly in the dark. "It's Broken Claw."

"What would she be doing here?"

"I don't know! This is not her valley. She dens one up, and she should be asleep in there now. Unless..."

"Unless what?"

She swore again. "Unless he's been luring her."

"Luring her? How?"

Silver didn't answer. She spun round, began moving fast, following bear spoor that now appeared to parallel their older tracks, left since early this morning.

Gabe's heart began to hammer, perspiration dampening him as he struggled to drag the horses behind him through thick snow, their hooves breaking through the crust, causing the animals to lag.

Silver crouched down, cursed again, lurched back to her feet, motioning for him to follow her back into the tree line. "Up this way."

There she stilled, her shoulders slumping. She dropped to her haunches, pointed. "It's another kill site," she said almost inaudibly,

Gabe studied the site with his flashlight. Blood, small bones, chunks of animal hair registered dark against white. It looked to him as if a small cat or rabbit had been eaten here.

"Her scat is full of fur and bone," Silver said as she got to her feet, her voice sounding suddenly drained. "He's been feeding her, Gabe. For days. Leaving little animals like this one to lure her behind him. She wouldn't do this on her own, not now. She'd be in hibernation. Easy food is keeping her out."

Silver stumbled out of the woods, and plunked herself down heavily in the snow. She buried her face into her gloves, shaking her head. "Why? Why would he do this?"

Gabe crouched down beside her. "The man is sick, Silver."

Snapping her head up, her eyes flared. "I can't do this, Gabe. He's messing with me."

Something inside her had given up. For Steiger, the hunt was as much about psychology as skill. Steiger's goal was to break the minds and the will of his prey, to see how long it took to do it. And whatever he was doing, it was working on Silver.

"Silver, what is it about this particular bear that's getting to you like this?"

She rubbed her gloves hard over her face, said nothing.

"Hey, talk through it, remember? We can do this together. A team. He wants to break us down, and we won't let him. So talk to me." He paused. "*Trust* me."

She stared into the distance for a while. "She's a good bear, Gabe," Silver said softly. "She was a good mother. Innocent and pure. I watched her with her cub when they first emerged from hibernation last spring." Her voice wobbled and she heaved out a gut-wrenching sigh, eyes filling with moisture.

He put his arm around her.

She sniffed, rubbed her nose with her sleeve. "I…I'm not used to being emotional, Gabe. I…I'm sorry. I don't know how to do it."

"Hey, it's okay. I'm here."

"He's destroying that bear, Gabe. He's forcing her to become habituated to humans, to associate them with food. She's got the taste of human blood now, because of that bastard. She's going to be dangerous. Violent. He's turning her into a man killer. Conservation will have to shoot her next summer. She'll be judged and punished for something that isn't her fault!"

"Why do you think Steiger would be doing this to her? How could he know how upsetting it is to you?

"I don't know!" She snapped. "Maybe he wants to force *me* to shoot her." She got to her feet. "Bloody bear is becoming a parallel to my own life."

"We should find safe shelter for the night, Silver," he said quietly. "You need some sleep. We need to find somewhere I can keep watch. We can pick up this trail again easily in first light."

His leg was bothering him too, pain from the metal pin becoming unbearable as the temperature plummeted. Wading through crusty snow was exacerbating the problem. He didn't want to tell her, but he suspected she'd noticed it herself.

If they were going to make it through a full day tomorrow, and perhaps face the Bush Man, they both needed rest. And he needed to understand what was breaking Silver down.

They'd tethered the horses and climbed up a small basalt cliff to a shallow cave on a rock ledge. Moonlight bathed the plains below, offering a good view.

Gabe had told Silver to curl up behind him and sleep, but she just sat there, knees drawn up tight, thinking of his words.

If we don't have trust, we have nothing.
Trust me, Silver.

She *had* to tell him. She couldn't hold off any longer. Her past was knotted into Steiger's game. Along with Gabe's future. If he didn't have all the facts, it could cost him his life.

Telling him might destroy her, but it also just might save him.

She closed her eyes, feeling the cold on her face, feeling the irony of sitting on a precipice.

She never thought she would love again. But Gabe Caruso had proved her wrong. She could no longer deny it—she had fallen in love with him, maybe even from that first moment she'd seen him step off that plane with that limp. He'd awakened her—emotionally and physically. He'd allowed her to begin to heal without threatening her privacy. He made her feel safe without challenging her autonomy. She felt strong with him. They were good as a team. And she knew in her heart that if it wasn't for her past, this was a man she could spend the rest of her life with.

But once she opened her mouth, everything would change. She sucked in a deep breath.

"Gabe, if you'd had the chance at Williams Lake…if that officer hadn't arrived when he did…would you have killed him?" she asked.

Gabe felt something cool and sinister, a dark shadow of wings across the moon as clouds began to whisper over the plains again. "You mean Steiger? When I'd tasered him?"

"Yes. After you'd tasered him, and before the other policeman got there, could you have murdered him? In the moment."

Gabe inhaled deeply. This place was raw, honest. He wanted to hide nothing. Not from her, nor from himself. "Yes," he said, quietly, telling her what he had kept from the psychologists. "I almost did. But my corporal arrived first."

She leaned closer, an edgy energy in her. Worry, unspecified, stole into him. "And if you had killed him? What then?"

"I didn't kill him."

"But if you had?"

A sense of impending dread whispered over his skin. "If it could be proven I hadn't acted purely in self-defense, then I'd have broken the law. I'd be doing time."

"Would that be fair?"

He looked out over the moonlit plains, fingering his rifle. "The law isn't always fair, Silver."

"But would you have hidden the truth, if you'd known you could get away with it? If there were absolutely no witnesses?"

He shot her a sharp look. "What are you getting at?"

She inhaled shakily. "Gabe…Steiger put that blood lure in the tree because somehow he knew that I did the same thing five years ago. To hide evidence."

A dark coldness swamped his gut.

"What evidence?"

A tear slid down her cheek. "I killed a man, Gabe."

His lungs squashed under a terrible crushing weight. He didn't trust himself to ask, didn't want to know. Terrified of what she was going to say, yet compelled to know more. He stared over the plain, gripping his rifle tight. Too tight.

"Who?" It came out hoarse. "Who did you kill, Silver?"

She looked away. "David Radkin. The father of my son."

Chapter 16

Gabe's entire world tilted.

"You'll find a record in the Black Arrow Falls detachment cold case files," she said softly. "The homicide team came up from Whitehorse to question me. But they couldn't pin anything on me. I...I didn't talk. And there was no evidence they could use. The blood lure attracted scavengers which destroyed most of what was left."

Christ.

He couldn't look at her. It was as if his head were being held in a vise.

She ripped open her jacket, exposing her scar. "Look at me, Gabe! *He* did this to me! He let my son drown. And when I found him wasted next to Johnny's little body, just lying out in the hot sun on the rocks, I—"

"Stop!"

He felt sick. He looked at her, his attention being torn from watching the land for Steiger below. She was white in the moonlight. Eyes huge. Vulnerable.

Gabe didn't know if he could trust his voice. "Silver, I...I'm a cop. You...you need to stop. Right here. Don't talk to me, don't tell me anything. Not without a lawyer. You need to do this with a lawyer."

Tears spilled down her face. She hugged her knees. Rocked back and forth. God, he wanted to know more. But what would he do then?

He was a Mountie, in uniform with sergeant's stripes. She was a civilian confessing to murder.

He'd have to bring her in. They'd reopen the Radkin file in conjunction with the Old Crow homicide. The rags alone would clue them in to the parallels. They'd question her.

If he didn't take her in, he'd be considered an accessory after the fact. His career would be over.

He got up, scrubbed his fingers over his face, hot in spite of the frigid chill. He stared down at her, a small brave figure, wan in the pale moonlight.

A shadow of sensation touched him, a cool whisper of evil. He glanced nervously over the valley, saw nothing moving. Then he knelt down beside Silver. He had to hear this through. He just had to, knowing at the same time the knowledge could be his downfall.

"Okay, tell me what happened. Everything. I need to know everything."

"Gabe...I..." She swallowed, eyes glimmering. "I just want you to understand, to forgive me."

"Talk to me, Silver," he said gently.

"When I found them, when I saw what had happened to my Johnny, I snapped. I confronted David—"

"With a weapon?"

"I...yes."

He cursed softly.

"I don't think I could have shot him dead at that point, but I wanted to make him suffer, make him bleed. But he over-powered me, threw me back on the river rocks, knocking me virtually senseless. He swore he was going to kill me. He called me terrible names, said I had ruined his life. He was high on something. Wild, unnaturally strong. He ripped my chest open with a jagged piece of rusted tin, and then…" she floundered, shaking. "He…raped me. Hurt me badly. Right within arm's reach of my dead child."

Gabe's stomach lurched, rage hardening every muscle in his body. His fingers tightened around the cold barrel of his gun, his world narrowing darkly.

"But before David could finish me off, before he could reach for his gun, I unsheathed my knife, dragged myself over, and I stabbed him. Under the ribs, angling up. A cut that would kill fast. I had no doubt he was going to shoot me." She went quiet.

He said nothing, wasn't sure what to think.

"It was self-defense, Gabe. You have got to believe that, in my heart, it was self-defense."

Gabe swore to himself. She'd be hard-pressed to prove it. If these confession details became part of the record, a Crown prosecutor would argue that she'd crawled over with the *intent* to kill while Radkin was unarmed and incapacitated. Her life was not under immediate threat at that point. She'd maybe get second degree, which carried an automatic life sentence. If she was lucky, she'd get away with manslaughter. Either way, she'd do time.

"Steiger somehow knows what happened at Wolverine Gorge, Gabe. He must have seen in the papers how they questioned me when David died, seen the press photo of the crime site with rags. Whether he thinks I killed David or not, he's using the rags to play a psychological game with me."

"Who found David's body?"

"A hunter came across what was left of his remains about two weeks later. He found the cairn of rocks where I buried Johnny, and the blood lure was still in the tree. It made the deaths suspicious. He called the Black Arrow Falls detachment, and homicide was flown up from Whitehorse."

"What made homicide question *you?*"

"I…I'd shot at David before."

"Oh, Jesus, Silver—"

"It was just a warning shot, when Johnny was two. I'd begun to see David for what he was, and I wanted him the hell out of my life. He threatened me, so I kept him off my property by firing to scare him. He tried to press assault charges, so that was the first time the cops talked to me. It was on record. So they thought I might have motive." She wavered. "They thought I could have killed my own son."

Gabe was dead silent, turning it over his mind, absently rubbing his thumb on the stock of his rifle as he stared out over the silver snowplain. "Why were you with this Radkin in the first place?" He needed to know, to understand.

She heaved out a breath. "He came to town when I was 18. My dad had recently died, and I was living in the cabin on my own. And David… He could be so charming. He had these incredible eyes, and smile, and nowhere to stay…and I'd never been with a guy, Gabe. He made me feel special. He moved in. He brought me presents each time he flew into Black Arrow Falls, and I didn't even think much about the bootlegging. It wasn't illegal. The band council has declared the town dry, and no one can sell liquor within town limits, but there's nothing to stop people from buying from outside. So David took orders, took their cash, and bought it for them, flew it in regularly. He'd get flats of beer and whiskey in Whitehorse, charter a plane. He said he was simply providing a needed service. It was only after I was pregnant that my blinders came off and I realized what he was really doing to my people. And by then he was bringing in harder stuff, too. And his personality was changing. Then one morning he struck me, just once, across the face. I told him get out, and to never come near me again. Nobody hits me, Gabe. I…I deserve better. My son deserved better."

His eyes burned with anger. Radkin had used her. So wise

in the ways of the wild, she'd been a virgin and innocent of the ways of a man like David Radkin.

"He came back again when Johnny was four. And that time the town helped keep him away from us. If the RCMP weren't going to stop him, then they would. They'd had enough of the destruction from booze. They didn't want him around."

Protecting their own, Gabe thought. Closing ranks. They must have seen from the get-go what he'd been doing to their Silver. Using her as a place to stay, a woman to bed on one of his many stops selling liquor to remote towns and First Nations across the North. Ferocity simmered low in his gut. "But he came back again five years ago and took your son?"

"I'll never know if it was to punish me. Or if part of him really wanted to be with his boy. I'll never know," she whispered.

"And that's why your scar wasn't stitched up properly—you didn't report the rape or the attack, did you?"

"I would have had to tell the police I was there. I…I would've had to stand trial, Gabe. An unsympathetic jury—" she cursed softly. "I did it in self-defense, and I know the courts might not see it that way. I've paid, Gabe. I have suffered. I have no child. I have a guilt that crushes my heart. Everything I do, every single day of my life, carries the fear of discovery." She swiped at the tears glistening over her cheeks. "A nurse at the clinic helped treat my injuries and the subsequent infection. The town helped me hide it from the police. The cops hadn't been there for me when I told them David had abducted my son. They couldn't stop David from doing what he was doing to the town with the booze. The police have *never* been there for me, Gabe. Their junior officers rotate every two years through Black Arrow Falls. They don't have a vested interest in us. They don't understand this place, its people, its ways, its history. How could I expect them to understand what had happened to *me?*"

So no report of Radkin's sexual assault on Silver had been filed. No examination of her injuries. No evidence left. It was now her word…against whose?

Silver's words whispered through his brain: *"Would you have hidden the truth if you'd known you could get away with it? If there were absolutely no witnesses?"*

He forced out the air trapped painfully in his chest. Had justice not been done? Had she not paid enough? What good would it do for the criminal justice system to punish her further? She wasn't a threat to society. There was no point in bringing this up again.

Ever.

Right now, he and Silver alone knew about those rags near Old Crow's body.

The photographs—he had taken pictures. Bury evidence? Gabe felt a sinister sickness sway though his body.

He was a cop.

He inhaled deeply. Where was that damn line? He'd crossed something within himself back in the snowy woods in Williams Lake over a year ago. He'd crossed that line further here in Black Arrow Falls when he'd embarked on this journey to hunt a man, knowing in the deepest crevices of his soul that if he found Steiger, he'd kill him.

Did that make him any different from her?

Maybe he was no longer fit to be a cop.

What the hell was retribution, anyway?

"Gabe…. I'm not asking you to choose between your duty and me. I know you have a sworn allegiance, and now you must do whatever you have to. But I did have to tell you. I never want to hide anything from you. And…more than anything I…I just want your forgiveness."

Tears choked her up. "I'm a good person, Gabe. I…I'm not bad. Of all people on this earth, I need you to understand that I am not a bad person." She was quiet for a few moments. "I love you, Gabe," she whispered.

He looked sharply up at the sky.

She loved him.

His eyes burned. He never thought he'd hear those words from a woman again. From Silver they carried more weight than she would ever know. She wasn't a woman to toy with things like this. If she said it, she meant it. He ached to touch, hold, just forget about everything. Tell her it would be all right. Erase her past.

But he couldn't.

He couldn't honestly promise it *would* be all right. She might not be asking him to make a choice, but he *did* have to make one. There was no middle ground here.

Silver had just given him the ultimate trust. She'd placed her life—her freedom—in his hands.

She'd also shaken his entire foundation—forcing him to question his own value system, his notion of justice and his personal role in law enforcement.

Gabe was a Mountie to the bones. His career was the fulfillment of a childhood dream, inspired by the history of the North. Now he was right here. In the North, under the stars, in his RCMP uniform.

And what did it mean?

What did it *really* mean?

He thought of the words of his own mentor, back at the depot in Regina where he'd trained as a young recruit all those years ago. *Never do anything, not even obey an order, if it conflicts with your sworn duty.*

Was his duty not to protect people like Silver? Had the system not let her down, driving her to seek retribution, to defend herself, on her own?

"Gabe?" He could hear her fear—fear that he was going to reject her.

He turned to her, but as he did, the horses whinnied softly down below. He tensed, held up his hand. Listened. He heard it again.

Gabe swore to himself. He'd been torn, distracted.

But before he could think, a high-velocity slug came walloping through the branches above them, slamming into the trunk, chunks and splinters of wood flying.

Silver grabbed her gun, but Gabe forced her flat onto the slab of stone, and they waited, tense. Another slug pounded and sparked off the rock overhang above them. Pieces of stone rained down on their heads.

Gabe motioned to Silver and they belly-crawled along the ledge, sliding over and ducking underneath it as another slug came from above, exploding into a tree trunk, shrapnel flying. Silver gasped as something caught her arm. Blood began to glisten through a jagged tear in her sleeve.

Gabe grabbed her good arm as another slug walloped into the rock behind him, and they scrambled, rolled, and cartwheeled wildly down the slope over sharp talus and through coarse thicket that tore at their clothes.

They got to the bottom, their breathing ragged.

The horses were gone.

He'd taken them.

Steiger had flushed Silver and Gabe out of their shallow cave like pheasants from grass, putting them on the run on foot. No horses, no gear.

This was his endgame—his ultimate thrill.

Silver was bleeding, holding her arm hard against her stomach. Gabe saw that it was her shooting hand. She was gripping her shotgun unsteadily in her left hand.

"Silver—"

"Go!" she whispered. "Keep moving, I'm okay. Run, damn it!"

They straggled through the snow, using the brush to cover them from above.

Gabe's knee was seizing up badly. He'd bashed his old injuries against sharp talus on the way down. Gabe dragged his leg as he and Silver stumbled over ice-packed drifts, breaking through the crust and sinking deep every few feet, wasting time and precious energy, Silver leaving blood on the snow each time she fell.

Where moonlight had given them an opportunity to see their foe coming for miles, it was now their enemy, highlighting their fleeing shapes against a glimmering platinum expanse.

Another shot thumped into the snow, shooting up crystals behind them.

It was just a matter of time before Steiger caught up to them. He had their horses, their supplies. Their tracks in the snow, the blood Silver was leaving were blazing beacons.

The next move was up to the Bush Man.

He lay flat on the cliff edge and sighted down the barrel, watching the two black shadows stumble and flee in the white moonlight.

He lowered his gun. Not yet.

He had better plans for them. First they must truly feel the fear. He needed them to feel desperate.

He scrambled to his feet, biting down suddenly on a bolt of pain that shot from his thigh into his groin. The infection was getting worse. But once he'd finished with Caruso and the tracker, he'd get over these mountains, make it into Alaska. From there, it would be just a short boat trip across the Bering Sea.

Once in Russia, he'd move south. No one would find him. He'd be free to hunt again.

Chapter 17

Steiger could have finished them off by now—if he'd wanted to. He was dragging it out, toying with them. Gabe ducked behind a rock, drawing Silver down beside him in the snow. She leaned back against the frozen stone, breathing hard. Her glove and sleeve were drenched with blood.

"We can't stop, Gabe. We've got to keep moving," she said between gasps for breath.

"I have to look at your arm."

"I just caught some shrapnel. I'm fine."

He could see that she wasn't. She was weakening, shivering from cold. He peered cautiously up over the rock, couldn't see any sign of Steiger up on the cliffs. Carefully, he removed her blood-soaked glove and pushed up her sleeve. His stomach tightened.

Large slivers of tree had embedded themselves in the flesh of her forearm and hand. He needed to remove them, disinfect her wounds. If they could make it up into the tunnels of the

Wolverine Mine, they could find shelter. He could get her warm, fix her up as best he could. And then come up with a plan.

At the same time Gabe knew that was probably exactly what Steiger figured they would do. He was going to trap them in the mine, like rats.

But they didn't have a choice. Their tracks were a beacon, and there was no imminent snowfall to cover them. The earlier wisps of cloud had moved on, and the sky was now clear as a bell.

They could at least hide deep in the shafts, perhaps until help came in three days. It was their last resort.

He took a cotton bandanna from his pocket, bound it tight around the worst part of her arm in an effort to apply pressure and stop further blood loss. "Come," he said. "I can look at it again in the mine."

"The river," she said, pointing to a creek, her breaths still short and shallow. "If we wade in the water we won't leave a trace."

Silver wasn't thinking with her usual crisp logic, and Gabe suddenly worried whether hypothermia might be slowing her mind.

"He'll see we went in here, Silver. Our prints will lead straight into the water, and it's obvious we'd head north in the creek, up to the mine from this point. We'll get wet and cold for nothing—"

She glanced up suddenly, a look of sheer horror crossing her face. Gabe spun round to see what had scared her.

Up on the frozen ridge stood the dark hulk of a bear. A grizzly, watching them silently from above.

"It's her," she whispered. "It's Broken Claw."

The grizz reared up on her hind legs, an awesome sight silhouetted against the silvery moonlight, her mouth open, tasting air. Tasting *them*.

"She's following us, Gabe. She has our scent."

Gabe glanced at Silver, at her bleeding hand, the way the

wind was blowing. A fist of tension curled tight inside him. Her blood was enticing the grizz.

"All Steiger has to do is follow the bear's movement along the ridge," she said. "He can probably see her for miles." Silver slumped back against the rock, defeated suddenly. "He did this, Gabe." She spoke so quietly he had to lean forward to hear. "He destroyed her." She watched Broken Claw up on the ridge. "She'll be punished now," she whispered. "She'll be shot and killed…"

"Silver—" Gabe crouched down besides her. "You can't keep thinking about that now. We need to keep moving. We *can't* let him win."

"He *has* won." Tears streamed silently down her face— tears she'd said she hadn't been able to shed until she met him. He'd made her vulnerable. He had made her open her heart and confess. He could not—would not—let her down now.

"No, Silver. He hasn't won. Not yet."

She didn't move.

"Hey." He cupped the side of her face, looking into her eyes. "I love you," he said softly. "I'm not going to let him take someone I love from me. Not again. And Silver, I'm going to protect you. After we get out."

She stared at him, eyes luminous. "What…what do you mean? You…*forgive me?*" Her voice was hoarse.

He tilted her chin. "It's not my place to forgive. You need to forgive yourself. I just want you to know, I trust you. I believe in you. And I love you."

She stared. Incredulous. A myriad of emotions crossing her face. Tears glistening in her eyes.

"See?" He forced a smile. "We do have a future to fight for. Don't give up on me. Not now. Not ever."

He reached out, grasped her good hand, helped her to her feet, and held tight for a moment.

"You won't turn me in?"

"It's not a matter of *won't,* Silver." He paused. *"I can't."*

He just couldn't. It wasn't about logic, or duty, or honor. It was about his heart. This place had stripped everything else away. That's all that was left. All that mattered.

"Thank you, Gabe," she whispered.

"No," he said softly, and kissed her gently, quickly. "Thank *you*."

The old mine lived up to its haunted reputation.

Bathed in cold moonlight and contrasted against snow, the black shapes of an abandoned ore crusher, a winch house, and the crumbling ruins of forsaken buildings squatted forbiddingly against the side of the mountain. The rusted boxes of a tramway creaked against an old steel cable in the icy breeze.

Gabe's flashlight probed into the pitch blackness of what appeared to be the main shaft entrance.

Shapes and shadows sprang out of the cold abyss to greet them. There was a pile of old creosote-treated sleepers near the entrance, a faint smell of gasoline that jangled warning bells in the back of Gabe's head. The shaft deepened into a warren of tunnels that ran out from the back of the cavern into the black heart of the mountain. Water dripped from long, milky icicles.

Gabe, ignoring the fierce pain in his own leg, treated Silver's hand and arm as best he could with the small first aid kit on his gun belt as she held the flashlight for him. He pulled out what slivers he could, wiped her wounds with disinfectant, and bandaged her up, but she'd lost a lot of blood and still had debris in there. The wound was swelling—her whole arm stiffening up to her shoulder, and he was worried about infection. She needed medical attention soon.

It was also her shooting arm.

She said she could manage with her left, but he knew she'd never make as good a shot, especially with the kick action of her twelve-gauge. Nevertheless, it remained her weapon of choice, and he left her guarding the front entrance with it as he made a quick reconnaissance of the back of their cave.

"Tunnels go off at all angles," he said as he returned. "Some dropping sharply. I went in a ways, but the air doesn't feel right. I'm worried about oxygen, other gases. I don't think it would be wise to go in much farther, if we can help it."

She nodded, eyes trained on the darkness outside. "Broken Claw's out there. I see her shadow in the rocks. Prowling."

He wondered where Steiger was prowling, what the game was to be.

"Do you think we'll make it out, Gabe?" she whispered. "Do you think we'll ever make it back?"

"We have to."

She glanced at him, and his heart twisted, his chest filling with emotion. "I want to spend my life with you, Silver. I need more than a few hours in an abandoned mine."

"You're giving me false hope."

"There's no such thing as false hope."

She smiled wryly.

They watched the darkness for a few moments, just the plop of water from the tips of icicles breaking the silence.

"Gabe," she said suddenly. "You're RCMP, I know how the Mounted Police work. If you're posted somewhere else in the country, you'll leave…they all do."

"Shh." He clamped his hand on her arm. "I heard someone, something."

A soft whirring reached his ears, accompanied by a streak of flickering orange light through the night—arcing toward their position. Gabe's adrenaline kicked into his heart as he recognized what it was.

Molotov cocktail!

He grabbed Silver's hand, dragging her at a wild stumbling run into the back of the cave just as the bottle exploded with a crack, spilling flames in a gushing whoosh over the old creosote beams.

Thick, acrid smoke began to billow into the cavern,

shadows shimmering and jumping and clawing at them from all directions, the scent vile.

"Cover your mouth!" he yelled. "We've got to get out of here, that stuff is toxic!"

"He's smoking us out!" Silver coughed, her arm over her mouth as they edged along the wall back towards the entrance of the shaft.

But as she leaned forward to take a gulp of fresh, icy air, a slug walloped into the rock beside her. She jerked back with a cry of shock, eyes watering from smoke.

They were either going to be overcome by the witch's brew of toxins and carbon monoxide filling their cavern as the chemically treated wood burned fierce, or, if they chose to flee the shaft, they were going to be picked off by Steiger playing sniper, hidden in the rocks outside.

"We've got to go into the back!" Gabe pulled her arm, covering his nose and mouth. "We have to go down into the tunnels!"

They ran in a crouch toward the first tunnel that dipped sharply forward into the darkness. It narrowed, the ceiling growing lower, the ground more uneven as they further penetrated the depths of the mountain, Gabe's flashlight throwing a pale, bouncing circle of light into the black hole as they ran.

Abruptly a boom shuddered through the mine. They dropped flat to the ground as bits of debris rained down on them and rocks tumbled and crashed in tunnels lower down.

A rumble, growing louder and louder, erupted from somewhere deep inside the bowels of the mountain, then a whoosh of dust and air exploded out at them.

They hunkered together, squeezing their eyes shut. Then all was quiet, apart from the skittering of small rocks and sand settling from the ceiling of the shaft.

Gabe opened his eyes, directed his light down the shaft. Dust floated in the beam. A creaking groan sounded as wooden supports stressed and shifted under the changed weight distribution. Then another deep rumble growled in the earth.

"Explosives," Gabe whispered. "He set explosives down one of the tunnels. Why?" Then a strange soft roar reached them, growing louder. "It sounds like a waterfall!" he said.

"Gabe—" Silver coughed into her sleeve.

He shot a look at her, not liking the tone of her voice.

She was covered in fine dust, her eyes huge, terrified.

She swallowed, holding his gaze. "It *is* a waterfall, Gabe" she whispered. "It's the tarn. He's ruptured the barrier wall between the mountain lake and the mine. There was an explosion years ago that exposed a latent geological fault in the granite barrier that held the water back from the tunnels. It's the reason they shut the mine down. It was too expensive to drain the lake when weighed against the dwindling yield."

He stared at her. "The whole lake could implode within minutes."

She nodded.

The sound grew even louder, a rushing, sloshing sound of water boiling up through the tunnels. The acrid smoke lay dense above.

They were trapped like bloody rats.

"Silver, think quick…what else do you know about this mine? You said your dad worked here. Did he ever talk about the tunnels, other ways out?"

She thought for a moment. "He brought me up here when I was a kid." Hope crept into her eyes suddenly. "I…I remember an entrance on the west side of the mountain."

Gabe checked his watch compass, hoping nothing underground was throwing the needle off true north. He could also read on his watch how deep in the earth they were. "We need to go down, that way." He grasped her hand.

"But the water—it's coming up!" she protested.

Another crushing explosion growled through the lower tunnels, dust flushing up as walls below crumbled and collapsed. "We *have* to go down if we want to go west. This shaft is our last hope, Silver. You with me?"

She nodded, features tight.

He picked up a long piece of wood lying on the ground to use as a cane. His leg was almost completely seized up with pain and cold. "Hold on to my jacket. Whatever you do, don't let go."

She grabbed onto him and they began to move as fast as they could, lower and in a westerly direction, according to Gabe's compass reading.

Then suddenly they hit a dead-end wall, and the tunnel veered sharply south and down. They stared in horror into the black hole.

Icy water was beginning to bleed up into their tunnel now, sloshing at their boots.

"We've got to take it," he said, leading her down into the southerly shaft, probing the floor under the water with his stick to judge depth. "It's got to turn west again."

"How do you know?"

He didn't. "Just trust me," he said. Frigid water began to lap at their ankles. He could feel his toes going numb. They tripped and stumbled as the tunnel floor grew uneven and the walls narrowed. Then without warning, Gabe's flashlight dimmed and cut out.

Blackness leapt at them, swallowed them whole.

He cursed. "Where's your flashlight, Silver?" he said, sound in the tunnel suddenly taking on different nuances in the blackness, the water more noisy at their feet.

"It's in my saddlebag. Oh, God, Gabe—"

He felt for her face, touched it. "Stay calm. Hold this." He shrugged out of his jacket and pushed it into her hands. He then felt for his knife on his duty belt. He hacked at his shirt sleeve, feeling his way blindly as he tore it free from his arm.

Water was rising faster, tugging at his pants around his calves now. He had to hurry.

He felt for the tiny personal survival kit on his duty belt, pulled out a tinder card. He wrapped his sleeve tight around the top of his stick, tucking the card underneath the fabric. Leaving a strip of fabric hanging loose on the end, he fumbled in the kit pouch for his butane lighter, and ignited the fabric. The tinder caught, and his improvised torch flared to life.

Flame flickered, shadows mocked, leered. They didn't have time to waste—the torch wouldn't burn for long. "This way," he said. Water swished, ice-cold, deeper as they slopped through the tunnel. The shaft narrowed some more, turned left.

And they met a wall.

Gabe tensed. They couldn't go back up. Steiger was there. Even if the smoke died down, he was waiting.

Another rumble sounded deep within the mine.

They really were trapped. His leg was now dead from cold, and he could feel Silver weakening. He felt for her hand, held it tight.

His flame was beginning to die. The air was close, not enough oxygen to sustain fire.

This was it. He looked at her and she at him.

The torch flickered suddenly, and Gabe waited for complete blackness. But it quivered again, sharply, flaring a little brighter.

Oxygen! It was drawing air from somewhere, feeding on it.

He moved in the direction the flame was leaping for. He could feel a soft breeze on his face now, and his heart began to pound. The tunnel curved. He checked his compass.

"We're heading west again."

Her hand tightened in his as she squeezed. Water was up to their thighs now, adding hypothermia to their list of worries.

Then they came to another dead end.

His stomach bottomed out. This place was a bloody labyrinth.

"Gabe," she whispered. "Look at the torch."

The flame was flaring again, burning straight up. "Up!" she said. "There's a shaft up there somewhere. There's got to be. Over here, look, a rung in the wall. This has got to lead out."

Gabe edged backwards, and craned his neck up into the blackness. He glimpsed a sight that made his heart soar—a tiny slice of sky with stars, way, way up.

He tugged on the metal rung affixed to the rock face, testing it with his full weight. It held. "You got a belt, Silver?"

He was worried about her being able to climb all that way with her injured arm, especially if the rest of her limbs felt as numb and uncooperative as his. She might not be able to hang on, fall.

She undid her leather belt. He looped it under her arms, buckled it across her chest, and hooked his arm into it. "I'm going to have to drop the torch, you ready for this?"

She nodded.

"Use your good arm, I'll do the rest."

Rung by rung, fighting the pain of cold, water surging up under them as tunnels crushed and collapsed under the full weight of the mountain tarn, they climbed up, toward the northern sky.

And nothing had ever looked so good in Gabe's life.

Silver collapsed on the snow. She couldn't move her arm. Her legs were numb from cold. Gabe crouched down beside her. Just his presence, his touch, gave her faith. Hope. The will to hold on. But more than anything it was his promise to protect her, his absolution, that kept her believing in a future. She wasn't ready to die. Not yet.

"Down there," he whispered. "I want you to try and crawl down into that gulley and aim your gun up at this shaft opening."

"What are you going to do?" Damn, her speech was coming out slurred, her brain slow. The cold was getting to her. Fast.

He unhooked his radio. "I'm going to pray that Steiger still has Donovan's radio on him. I'm going to send a distress call to dispatch."

"They won't hear—we're out of range."

"They don't have to. It's fake—for him. I'm going to alert him to the fact we're at this mine shaft, and need help. But I'll be up on that ridge, waiting, and you'll be down in the gulley, covering the entrance from there. We ambush him. When you have him in your sights…" he paused. "Shoot to kill, Silver. Do not hesitate."

"Gabe, he'll know we're out of radio range. He'll suspect something."

"Yes, but he might also believe his quarry is desperate enough to try and call for help anyway. I know him. He'll come."

Gabe lay flat on the icy ridge, cheek to stock, sighting down the barrel, moonlight once again his friend. He watched Steiger's black shape moving cautiously along the far rocks, toward the west mine shaft entrance. His enemy. Pure evil. The man who had ripped open the lives of so many, who had destroyed Gia.

His finger twitched against the trigger. Gabe reminded himself to control his rage, to control his impulse to shoot, but seeing Steiger again so close was unnerving.

Steiger moved behind a wood structure, came out the other side, sifting between shadows, silhouetted like a black ghost against the snow. The moonlight caught him for a brief instant in a freeze frame. He was tall, six-foot-two, and solid, with a powerful posture, just as Silver had deduced from the prints he'd left near Old Crow's body. His pale hair gleamed an eerie silver in the lunar light, and he'd grown a beard. Gabe's heart thudded in his ears. He needed a cleaner shot. He'd only get one. If he missed, Steiger would duck down, and the game would be on—and he'd have squandered his only advantage. Steiger moved stealthily back into shadow, Gabe following with his sights.

Abruptly, another shape materialized in Gabe's peripheral vision. He flicked his eyes slightly to the side, tensed.

The bear!

She was on the rise above the gulley Silver was hiding in, moving lower down, cautiously, but straight toward Silver. She'd caught the scent of the blood on Silver's clothes.

Gabe's mouth went bone dry.

Silver hadn't seen the bear. From his vantage point, Gabe could see that Silver's eyes were trained solely on the shadow of Steiger who was creeping ever closer to the mine shaft.

If he shot at the bear, he'd alert Steiger, while maybe just enraging the animal. He'd seen what Silver's warning shot had done to the grizz up on Old Crow's plateau.

Steiger suddenly ducked behind a rock. *He'd seen their tracks!* He could see which way Silver had gone into the gulley, and he was now backtracking to come around at a point above her.

Adrenaline coursed through Gabe's blood.

He'd lost his shot.

He scrambled quietly, quickly down the snowbank, running in a crouch behind a ridge of rock that loomed over the shaft entrance. He came round the other side, picked up a small lump of icy snow, threw it behind Silver. It skittered down toward her.

She spun round, and saw the bear above her—and Steiger to her left.

Steiger raised his weapon, shouldering the stock, aiming dead at her.

Silver fired with her bad arm, her shot going wild, heavy-load buckshot slamming into snow to his left.

The Bush Man sighted down his barrel.

Gabe hesitated. Even if he hit him, Steiger might still manage to get off one shot. Silver was as good as dead.

"Steiger!" Gabe yelled, suddenly lurching to his feet, gun held out at his side, his other arm wide. "I'm the one you want. Here I am!"

Steiger faltered, taken by surprise. He swung his weapon toward Gabe—and fired. Gabe dove, catching his shoulder as his heel hit ice, shooting his feet out from under him. He grasped wildly for purchase, his weapon clattering down over rock, bouncing all the way down the slope behind him.

Gabe prayed that Silver had used the distraction to crawl away.

She hadn't.

He righted himself, drew his 9 mm, useless from this range, as she raised her shotgun again and pulled the trigger before the Bush Man had swung round to aim at her.

Silver's shot slammed into the top of Steiger's shoulder. The impact wheeled him round, blood and bone spattering outward as he lurched to the side. Then, startlingly, with a gaping wound and a flaccid arm, he staggered back onto his feet, and dropped behind a rusted old cart for protection.

Gabe scrambled behind a rock as Silver rolled herself like a rag doll lower into the gulley.

They were caught in a standoff.

Gabe had to find a way to get behind Steiger.

Then Gabe saw the bear cresting the ridge. He hadn't been aware of the grizz during the shootout. The animal must have been mildly startled by the gunfire and retreated slightly. But she was back, and now irate, pawing ground, scenting fresh, warm blood—Steiger's blood—glistening black on the snow in the moonlight.

He hadn't seen the bear return. She was behind and above him, looming like a dark, primal, shadow of death.

Steiger peered out from the side of the cart, taking aim at Silver down in the gulley. She was struggling to crawl behind a rock.

Gabe's heart froze.

But as Steiger raised his weapon, the grizz dropped onto all fours and barreled down the ridge. Five hundred pounds of flesh, bone, teeth and claws aided by the force of gravity exploded down the mountainside and slammed into the Bush Man.

An inhuman scream, raw, roared though the air, echoing, over and over again through the frozen granite mountains. A gunshot echoed, going wild.

Gabe stood in shock.

Then suddenly everything was silent. Still. Somewhere in the back of Gabe's mind, he noticed the northern lights billowing in a surreal curtain of light across the sky, the moon full, the stars bright, the heavens oblivious to the human drama below.

He scrambled, slid, and tumbled his way down the hill to Silver. He gathered her into his arms, holding her tight, and fierce passion burned his eyes. "We're going to make it, Silver," he whispered hoarsely. "We're going to get home."

She looked up, meeting his gaze. "I know."

Chapter 18

It had been five days since Gabe and Silver had departed Black Arrow Falls and trekked into the teeth of a storm in pursuit of the notorious survivalist serial killer.

The sun was bright.

A raven wheeled high in the piercing blue sky, watching the strange convoy they made in the snow below.

Their three horses cut single file across the white landscape, leaving a well-defined trail. Gabe and Silver rode the first two horses. Behind the third, strapped onto a sled crudely fashioned from timber found in the old Wolverine Mine, was the body of the Bush Man.

The hunt was over.

The hunters, wounded warriors, were returning home to their village. They'd left with secrets between them. They were coming back as a team.

Gabe had decided that what the world didn't know about Silver's past wouldn't hurt anyone. He would hide nothing from the authorities about the physical events of these last few days. But what had transpired between himself and Silver would remain between them.

Her secret was now his.

It was an ultimate trust. A bond of freedom. And to his mind, that was sacred.

What was past was just that—past.

It was now time to look to the future.

Their convoy traveled slowly over the undulating expanse of shimmering ice crystals, the mood quiet. They had built a fire, dried their clothes, warmed up. They'd eaten, and Gabe had redressed Silver's wounds. He'd fashioned the sled to transport what remained of Steiger, and when they felt stronger, they'd set out for home.

The raven high in the sky dipped his wings suddenly, and swept away as the sound of choppers thudded into the clear northern sky.

Three machines loomed shining on the horizon, making a beeline for the convoy trail the pilots could see from the air.

Help had come.

Gabe reached his arm up and waved.

Silver, however, turned to watch the raven wheeling away into the sky, and she knew that somewhere, Old Crow was watching her. And he was at peace.

Upon their return, they gradually learned the details of Steiger's journey to Black Arrow Falls.

A pilot and his small plane had gone missing from Dawson City almost two weeks before. His wife told Dawson RCMP that her husband had taken a charter north, but midflight had switched his destination to a point south—and never arrived.

Sonar showed a plane matching the description of the missing Beaver outlined at the bottom of Wolverine Lake, not far from the old mine. When the wreckage was hauled to the surface, it was apparent that the single-engine prop had been stripped of fuel and other basics. The pilot had been sunk with his ship, naked and strapped to his seat, his throat slit. His craft matched the description of the small red plane Gabe had seen struggling northwest of Black Arrow Falls.

Steiger had been wearing the pilot's clothes. The pilot's wife said her husband had a keen interest in the old gold mines of the North, and likely would have told Steiger about the geological fault at Wolverine Mine. He talked about the mines incessantly, to whomever would listen. The assumption was that Steiger had hijacked the plane from Dawson and used the information he'd gleaned about the mine fault in an effort to trap and terrorize Silver and Gabe.

Explosives had also been reported stolen from a construction site near Dawson. And police began to look differently at the case of a missing Dawson City librarian whose mutilated body had been found by dogs in the forest not far from the town.

The librarian who had been working with the murdered woman the day she had mysteriously vanished from her post at the library desk was shown photos of Kurtz Steiger. She said a man resembling him had been working on the computers the morning her colleague vanished. A computer forensics expert was brought in to examine the station he had used. It showed that Steiger had searched for information on Black Arrow Falls, and then narrowed his search down to articles on Silver, and then to David Radkin's death.

Investigators assumed he'd used the blood lure in the tree to unsettle her psychologically, because of her son and her son's father's deaths. Gabe added nothing more. Silver remained silent.

Media attention was intense, and focused entirely on the fact that the Bush Man's reign of terror had finally ended. Gabe and Silver were being touted as heroes, their aversion to the publicity only heightening their mystique.

But it was over.

The homicide team had left town. So had the media crews.

Business in Black Arrow Falls was returning to normal as the winter settled in with a vengeance.

The snows Gabe had thought might just end up killing him, had instead liberated him. There was something about the white cold that made the Yukon vistas seem more vast and clean and wild. And Silver was teaching him how to run a sled with dogs. Gabe had begun to think that maybe his childhood dreams were more about the North than about being a cop, and in so many ways he felt as if he'd found home.

Silver stood in the doorway to his office now, something wrapped in an Indian blanket bundled in her arms. The twinkle in her cobalt eyes was mischievous, a flicker of a secret curling her lips into a smile.

"Hey," she said, looking at him in her direct way.

His heart swelled with warmth. With pride. He got up from his desk. "What have you got in there?"

"It's for you. A present."

He peeled back the corner of the blanket, exposing a bundle of dirty-white fluff. Two beady little blue eyes looked out at him. He shot her a look.

"What's this?"

"It's Valkoinen's," she said, grinning broadly at his obvious surprise. "He sired a litter before he died. This little guy looks the most like his dad. He's yours."

"Why?"

Her features turned serious. "Because, Sergeant, you'll have to look after him. Because he loves the snow. And he's born to run in the North, and he has a wild streak like his father." Her eyes narrowed. "Because you can't take him away from this place, Gabe, and he might make you stay."

"Silver, I *am* going to stay."

"What if the job doesn't work out? What if they transfer you?"

"Come—" He grabbed his coat and they went out into the snow. Flakes swirled from the opaque sky, settling like soft bridal confetti on her shining black hair. He tucked the puppy into his jacket, zipping it up as he waved to Edith who was shaking a mat outside the general store.

He took Silver's arm as another villager passed by and called out a greeting to them in Gwitchin.

Gabe was welcome here now. He was becoming part of this larger family. He wasn't going anywhere.

He'd finally come home.

Donovan was out of the woods healthwise and back at work on limited duty, and Annie Lavalle and Stan Huong had also returned. Gabe had discovered he had a great team in them. Annie, with her fiery gold Arcadian eyes and fierce determination, her bright, easy smile; Stan with his strong Canadian-Asian looks and sharp logical mind. Donovan with his skill for handling people. Gabe could see working with them, mentoring them, for some time to come.

"I was offered a transfer," he said as they walked, boots squeaking in fresh powder. "A senior position with the major crimes unit in the lower mainland of BC."

She stopped dead. "You didn't tell me!"

"I'm telling you now. I turned it down. I'm not going anywhere, Silver. Why do you find that so hard to believe?"

She glanced down. "Maybe I just can't believe I found you," she said softly. "Maybe I'm scared because nothing ever really worked out for me."

He led her under a tree, out of the path of two snowmobiles.

"I wanted to do this differently, but I think now is the time." He paused, looking into her eyes. "Will you marry me, Silver? Will you be my wife? *Can* you be my wife—" God, now his heart was racing. "Could you possibly marry a cop?"

Her eyes turned luminous. The one man she thought would take her freedom away had given it to her completely.

And he would guard it with his life. This was a bold, powerful, and gentle man who would kill to keep her and her family safe, and she adored him for it.

She always thought she was strong alone. But with Gabe, she was stronger.

The puppy peeked out from his jacket.

"I need you," he said simply.

She looked into his warm Italian eyes, thinking of his extended family, his nurturing warmth, his belief in home and community. She couldn't believe she could possibly be part of something so much bigger.

"I'm worried, Gabe," she said quietly. "I'm worried that even though you've turned down the posting, this position at the detachment won't be there forever. I know how the RCMP works. What...what then?"

"Then I hand in my uniform, Silver,"

"You can't. It's who you are."

He shook his head. "No. You showed me who I am. Out there in the wilderness you made me confront what I was made of. You made me question my values."

"What would you do up here if you left law enforcement?"

He grinned wickedly.

"Oh...what?" She hit his arm. "You've been plotting something!"

He shrugged, eyes gleaming. "Maybe."

"Tell me!"

He inhaled deeply, looked down at the puppy's head, stroked it gently with his large strong hand. Then he met her eyes.

"We will run the best damn tracking school in North America, Silver. You and me. Right here. In Johnny's honor. We'll set up a foundation, bring in whatever expertise we need. We—you—can train law enforcement, search-and-rescue organizations—in the techniques you've learned from the wild. We'll have a special component focusing on missing children."

Her stomach swooped, her chest aching as his vision caught fire inside her. Her eyes filled with emotion. "How...how long have you been scheming this?"

"Since that first day back in the Old Moose Lodge bar. You told me they were tracking Steiger wrong. Remember? Something stuck in my mind. It made me think we could all look at things another way every now and then." He held her eyes. "You could show them how. And I could help you."

She went silent. Then very quietly, she said, "Old Crow would like that."

They married in the small Black Arrow Falls chapel the following winter.

Gabe's old partner, Tom, was his best man.

The media had been asked to be respectful, to keep it private.

But Gabe's entire family was there, and Silver's nation of Black Arrow came out in full force.

His heart swelled as he watched his bride approach. Her hair shimmered like the feathers of a raven in the sun. She wore a white velvet gown that the elder women had embroidered with small beads and feathers along the edges.

She had chosen winter to marry, her favorite time of the year.

Their dogs, Aumu, Lassi, and Valkoinen the Second—as Gabe had named their new puppy—milled behind her as she walked through the snow to the chapel entrance.

Gabe stood in his formal red serge, his shoulders square, his Stetson under his arm, his high boots and Sam Browne belt polished to a proud gleam.

Members from the Black Arrow Falls RCMP detachment, along with officers from Williams Lake, wore their formal scarlet uniforms, too. And they held an arch of Canadian flags, red and white, for Silver and Gabe to pass under.

Indian drums sounded as he reached for his bride's hand. He closed his fingers around hers and looked into her striking blue eyes. She was his compass. His true north. She'd showed him the way home.

An Indian chant—an old wedding song—accompanied the beat of drums as they walked into the chapel under the arch of flags, and Gabe's mother wept.

An old monsignor from Gabe's hometown Italian quarter—a friend of the Caruso family—married them in front of the small altar as the snow came down heavily beyond the long pane of stained glass.

From there, the party traipsed through the snow to Old Moose Lodge, children and dogs in tow.

The elders served up a traditional Black Arrow feast. Jake Onefeather and Chief Harry Peters served the drinks. And afterward, late into the night, Edith Josie's son played the fiddle as the town celebrated a marriage of the north.

Silver looked up into her Mountie's eyes, and her heart swelled. She'd known the instant he stepped off that plane and onto the dusty tarmac that this man was going to be trouble.

She just didn't know how much.

Or how worth it that trouble would be.

Silver leaned over and whispered in his ear, "I love you, Gabriel Caruso. You set me free, you know that?"

He smiled, eyes shimmering, and he gathered his bride tightly into his arms. "And you showed me the way home, Silver," he said, tilting her chin up. He kissed her on the mouth, the world fading away as the snow swirled thick outside.

* * * * *

Look for the next story in Loreth Anne White's
exciting new miniseries,
WILD COUNTRY
Coming soon to Silhouette Romantic Suspense.

Here is a sneak preview of
A STONE CREEK CHRISTMAS,
the latest in Linda Lael Miller's acclaimed
MCKETTRICK *series.*

A lonely horse brought vet Olivia O'Ballivan to Tanner
Quinn's farm, but it's the rancher's love that might cause
her to stay.

A STONE CREEK CHRISTMAS
Available December 2008
from Silhouette Special Edition

Tanner heard the rig roll in around sunset. Smiling, he wandered to the window. Watched as Olivia O'Ballivan climbed out of her Suburban, flung one defiant glance toward the house and started for the barn, the golden retriever trotting along behind her.

Taking his coat and hat down from the peg next to the back door, he put them on and went outside. He was used to being alone, even liked it, but keeping company with Doc O'Ballivan, bristly though she sometimes was, would provide a welcome diversion.

He gave her time to reach the horse Butterpie's stall, then walked into the barn.

The golden retriever came to greet him, all wagging tail and melting brown eyes, and he bent to stroke her soft, sturdy back. "Hey, there, dog," he said.

Sure enough, Olivia was in the stall, brushing Butterpie down and talking to her in a soft, soothing voice that touched something private inside Tanner and made him want to turn on one heel and beat it back to the house.

He'd be damned if he'd do it, though.

This was *his* ranch, *his* barn. Well-intentioned as she was, *Olivia* was the trespasser here, not him.

"She's still very upset," Olivia told him, without turning to look at him or slowing down with the brush.

Shiloh, always an easy horse to get along with, stood contentedly in his own stall, munching away on the feed Tanner had given him earlier. Butterpie, he noted, hadn't touched her supper as far as he could tell.

"Do you know anything at all about horses, Mr. Quinn?" Olivia asked.

He leaned against the stall door, the way he had the day before, and grinned. He'd practically been raised on horseback; he and Tessa had grown up on their grandmother's farm in the Texas hill country, after their folks divorced and went their separate ways, both of them too busy to bother with a couple of kids. "A few things," he said. "And I mean to call you Olivia, so you might as well return the favor and address me by my first name."

He watched as she took that in, dealt with it, decided on an approach. He'd have to wait and see what that turned out to be, but he didn't mind. It was a pleasure just watching Olivia O'Ballivan grooming a horse.

"All right, *Tanner*," she said. "This barn is a disgrace. When are you going to have the roof fixed? If it snows again, the hay will get wet and probably mold…"

He chuckled, shifted a little. He'd have a crew out there the following Monday morning to replace the roof and shore up the walls—he'd made the arrangements over a week before—but he felt no particular compunction to explain that. He was enjoying her ire too much; it made her color rise and her hair fly when she turned her head, and the faster breathing made her perfect breasts go up and down in an enticing rhythm. "What makes you so sure I'm a greenhorn?" he asked mildly, still leaning on the gate.

At last she looked straight at him, but she didn't move from Butterpie's side. "Your hat, your boots—that fancy red truck you drive. I'll bet it's customized."

Tanner grinned. Adjusted his hat. "Are you telling me real cowboys don't drive red trucks?"

"There are lots of trucks around here," she said. "Some of them are red, and some of them are new. And *all* of them are splattered with mud or manure or both."

"Maybe I ought to put in a car wash, then," he teased. "Sounds like there's a market for one. Might be a good investment."

She softened, though not significantly, and spared him a cautious half smile, full of questions she probably wouldn't ask. "There's a good car wash in Indian Rock," she informed him. "People go there. It's only forty miles."

"Oh," he said with just a hint of mockery. "*Only* forty miles. Well, then. Guess I'd better dirty up my truck if I want to be taken seriously in these here parts. Scuff up my boots a bit, too, and maybe stomp on my hat a couple of times."

Her cheeks went a fetching shade of pink. "You are twisting what I said," she told him, brushing Butterpie again, her touch gentle but sure. "I meant…"

Tanner envied that little horse. Wished he had a furry hide, so he'd need brushing, too.

"You *meant* that I'm not a real cowboy," he said. "And you could be right. I've spent a lot of time on construction sites over the last few years, or in meetings where a hat and boots wouldn't be appropriate. Instead of digging out my old gear, once I decided to take this job, I just bought new."

"I bet you don't even *have* any old gear," she challenged, but she was smiling, albeit cautiously, as though she might withdraw into a disapproving frown at any second.

He took off his hat, extended it to her. "Here," he teased. "Rub that around in the muck until it suits you."

She laughed, and the sound—well, it caused a powerful and wholly unexpected shift inside him. Scared the hell out of him and, paradoxically, made him yearn to hear it again.

* * * * *

*Discover how this rugged rancher's wanderlust is tamed
in time for a merry Christmas, in
A STONE CREEK CHRISTMAS.
In stores December 2008.*

Silhouette

SPECIAL EDITION™

FROM *NEW YORK TIMES* BESTSELLING AUTHOR

LINDA LAEL MILLER

A STONE CREEK CHRISTMAS

Veterinarian Olivia O'Ballivan finds the animals in Stone Creek playing Cupid between her and Tanner Quinn. Even Tanner's daughter, Sophie, is eager to play matchmaker. With everyone conspiring against them and the holiday season fast approaching, Tanner and Olivia may just get everything they want for Christmas after all!

Available December 2008 wherever books are sold.

THE ITALIAN'S BRIDE

Commanded—to be his wife!

Used to the finest food, clothes and women, these immensely powerful, incredibly good-looking and undeniably charismatic men have only one last need: a wife!

They've chosen their bride-to-be and they'll have her—willing or not!

Enjoy all our fantastic stories in December:

THE ITALIAN BILLIONAIRE'S SECRET LOVE-CHILD
by CATHY WILLIAMS (Book #33)

SICILIAN MILLIONAIRE, BOUGHT BRIDE
by CATHERINE SPENCER (Book #34)

BEDDED AND WEDDED FOR REVENGE
by MELANIE MILBURNE (Book #35)

THE ITALIAN'S UNWILLING WIFE
by KATHRYN ROSS (Book #36)

www.eHarlequin.com   HPE1208

Silhouette®

nocturne™

New York Times bestselling author

MERLINE LOVELACE

LORI DEVOTI

———

HOLIDAY WITH A VAMPIRE II

**CELEBRATE THE HOLIDAYS WITH TWO
BREATHTAKING STORIES FROM
NEW YORK TIMES BESTSELLING AUTHOR
MERLINE LOVELACE AND LORI DEVOTI.**

Two vampires, each wary of human relationships,
are put to the test when holiday encounters blur
the boundaries of passion and hunger.

Available December wherever books are sold.

SN61801

REQUEST YOUR
FREE BOOKS!

2 FREE NOVELS PLUS 2 FREE GIFTS!

Silhouette® Romantic

SUSPENSE

Sparked by Danger, Fueled by Passion!

YES! Please send me 2 FREE Silhouette® Romantic Suspense novels and my 2 FREE gifts (gifts are worth about $10). After receiving them, if I don't wish to receive any more books, I can return the shipping statement marked "cancel." If I don't cancel, I will receive 4 brand-new novels every month and be billed just $4.24 per book in the U.S. or $4.99 per book in Canada, plus 25¢ shipping and handling per book plus applicable taxes, if any*. That's a savings of at least 15% off the cover price! I understand that accepting the 2 free books and gifts places me under no obligation to buy anything. I can always return a shipment and cancel at any time. Even if I never buy another book from Silhouette, the two free books and gifts are mine to keep forever.

240 SDN EEX6 340 SDN EEYJ

Name _____ (PLEASE PRINT)

Address _____ Apt. # _____

City _____ State/Prov. _____ Zip/Postal Code _____

Signature (if under 18, a parent or guardian must sign) _____

Mail to the Silhouette Reader Service:
IN U.S.A.: P.O. Box 1867, Buffalo, NY 14240-1867
IN CANADA: P.O. Box 609, Fort Erie, Ontario L2A 5X3

Not valid to current subscribers of Silhouette Romantic Suspense books.

Want to try two free books from another line?
Call 1-800-873-8635 or visit www.morefreebooks.com.

* Terms and prices subject to change without notice. N.Y. residents add applicable sales tax. Canadian residents will be charged applicable provincial taxes and GST. Offer not valid in Quebec. This offer is limited to one order per household. All orders subject to approval. Credit or debit balances in a customer's account(s) may be offset by any other outstanding balance owed by or to the customer. Please allow 4 to 6 weeks for delivery. Offer available while quantities last.

Your Privacy: Silhouette is committed to protecting your privacy. Our Privacy Policy is available online at www.eHarlequin.com or upon request from the Reader Service. From time to time we make our lists of customers available to reputable third parties who may have a product or service of interest to you. If you would prefer we not share your name and address, please check here. ☐

SRS08R

Silhouette® Romantic
SUSPENSE

COMING NEXT MONTH

#1539 BACKSTREET HERO—Justine Davis
Redstone, Incorporated

When Redstone executive Lilith Mercer is nearly injured in two suspicious accidents, her boss calls in security expert Tony Alvera. But the street-tough, too-attractive *younger* agent is the last man Lilith wants protecting her as she faces her tarnished past. They get closer to the truth, and find that danger—and love—are hiding in plain sight.

#1540 SOLDIER'S SECRET CHILD—Caridad Piñeiro
The Coltons: Family First

They'd shared one night of passion eighteen years ago, but Macy Ward had never told anyone that Fisher Yates was the father of her son, T.J. Now Fisher is back in town, and when T.J. disappears, Macy turns to him for help. Will their search for their son reveal the passion they've been denying all these years?

#1541 MERRICK'S ELEVENTH HOUR—Wendy Rosnau
Spy Games

Adolf Merrick—code name Icis—has discovered a mole in the NSA Onyxx Agency, which has allowed his nemesis to stay one step ahead. In a plot to capture his enemy, Merrick kidnaps the man's wife—who mysteriously has his own dead wife's face! With the clock ticking and the stakes high, Merrick is in a race against time for the truth.

#1542 PROTECTED IN HIS ARMS—Suzanne McMinn
Haven

Amateur psychic Marysia O'Hurley figures her powers are the real deal when U.S. Marshal Gideon Brand enlists her help. The reluctant allies embark on a roller-coaster ride to rescue a little girl, with killers one step behind them. Even as they dodge bullets, will they find passion in each other's arms?

SRSCNMBPA1108